D0506362

DOCTOR·WHO

The Slitheen Excursion

DOCTOR·WHO

The Slitheen Excursion

SIMON GUERRIER

BOOKS

2 4 6 8 10 9 7 5 3 1

Published in 2009 by BBC Books, an imprint of Ebury Publishing.
Ebury Publishing is a division of the Random House Group Ltd.

Doctor Who is a BBC Wales production for BBC One
Executive Producers: Russell T Davies and Julie Gardner

The Random House Group Ltd Reg. No. 954009.
Addresses for companies within the Random House Group can be found at
www.randomhouse.co.uk.

A CIP catalogue record for this book is available from the British Library.

ISBN 978 1 846 07640 4

The Random House Group Limited supports the Forest Stewardship
Council (FSC), the leading international forest certification organisation.
All our titles that are printed on Greenpeace approved FSC certified
paper carry the FSC logo. Our paper procurement policy can be found
at www.rbooks.co.uk/environment

Series Consultant: Justin Richards
Project Editor: Steve Tribe
Cover design by Lee Binding © BBC 2009

Typeset in Albertina and Deviant Strain
Printed and bound in Germany by GGP Media GmbH, Poessneck

For my mother-in-law

Wild dogs roamed the streets outside the Acropolis, the huge, high rock overlooking Athens. Their claws skittered on the smooth marble flagstones, and their tongues lolled from between snaggled, yellow teeth. They looked hungry and bedraggled, and they kept most people away from the ancient monument in the hours before it opened.

June pretended not to notice the scraggy, smelly things as they trotted back and forth around her. She remembered what her ex-boyfriend had taught her about big dogs; she didn't make eye contact with them, she kept her arms folded, her fingers out of sight, and she kept on walking, despite the weight of her rucksack. It seemed to work. The dogs tagged along expectantly but didn't try to eat her.

The sun sat low in the early-morning sky, honey-coloured sunlight burnishing the trees. The air smelt fresh and of pine needles. Away down the hill behind her, Athens came slowly to life, the distant burble of cars and chatter echoing up the hill. Up here, all was silent but for the dogs' eager breathing. But one by one even they left her alone, padding dolefully away to scrounge easier pickings.

June made her way to the ticket kiosk. A large man sat up behind the glass partition, eyes fixed on his newspaper. Just as she had ignored the dogs, so the man ignored June. She stuck her tongue out at him and crossed her eyes until a split second before he looked up. Then she smiled her most winning smile. He sighed, looked at his watch and returned to his paper. June dumped her rucksack down on the floor, her shoulders aching, and waited.

At one minute past eight in the morning, he tucked his newspaper away and slid the glass partition open to peer down at her.

'*Boro na eho esitirio parakalo?*' said June, her accent not half bad after two weeks' practice.

The man scrutinised her student ID, then unhurriedly tore off a ticket from the book in front of him. He muttered the price so quietly no sound actually escaped his lips, but June already had the correct change in euros. The man seemed to find this exhausting.

'*Efharisto,*' said June sweetly. Heaving her bag back onto her shoulders, she made her way up the pathway behind the kiosk.

At the gate, a guard with a twinkle in his eye tore her ticket. He made a joke she didn't quite understand as he handed it back to her. June could ask for food and drink and hotel rooms fluently, but she wasn't up to flirting. She just smiled at him, tolerant but not encouraging, and continued on her way. In just over two hours she'd be on a train heading back to St Pancras. Why did men only ever show an interest when it was too late?

The path led her up to some steep, marble steps, the ancient remains of an impressive entrance gateway. June climbed the steps, her heart pounding not with the effort but with anticipation. High above her loomed the Propylea. The marble blazed white in the early-morning sun.

She reached the top of the steps and halted. Before her, up the gentle rise of bare rock, stood the Parthenon, the ruined, sun-bleached temple that had overlooked Athens for two and a half thousand years. June gazed at it in awe, despite having seen it three times in as many days. Again, she let her eyes pick over the details, her brain alive with all the history and myth she'd gleaned from her reading.

The Parthenon had been built before the invention of the load-bearing arch, so the huge, tall columns had to jostle close together to hold up the roof. Not that there was a roof any more; it had been destroyed in an explosion of gunpowder in 1687. The temple's vivid sculptures had then found their way into various museums and private collections. These scant fragments, scattered around the world, gave a tantalising glimpse of the ancient people who'd once lived and worshipped here. But, like a jigsaw with half the pieces missing, only a small part of the picture remained. Students like June used the hotchpotch of remaining fragments to guess at the distant past.

The temple and its sculptures would have been painted in bright colours, the air alive with scented smoke and music. To the left of the temple would have stood an enormous statue of Athene, goddess of wisdom, who had given her name to the city. According to myth, she and the god Poseidon had competed for the honour, offering gifts to the people to win their favour. Poseidon had offered their sailors calm waters; Athene had planted an olive tree.

Whatever the truth of the story, ancient Athens had made its money trading olive oil. It had grown so rich the citizens had lived comfortably, with enough leisure time to invent the structures of drama and democracy still recognised in the world today. In fact, June knew, everything from modern maths to medicine owed a debt to the ancient Greeks.

So the spot on which she stood was in some ways the birthplace of the world she knew. She boggled at the thought, resisting the need to check her watch to count down the minutes she had left here. Another hour and she'd have to lug her rucksack down to the train station for the long journey home to England. June had wanted one last quiet moment with this extraordinary place before her holiday was over. But she didn't have it to herself for long.

A coach party of fat, noisy tourists made their way up the steps behind her. June quickly got out of their way, following the gravel pathway round the side of the Parthenon. In the two weeks she had been in Athens, she had learnt to despair of other tourists. They stopped to take or pose in photographs, but not to simply look at the monuments. She wanted to tell them to slow down, to shut up, to think about where they were. But these people were bustling around the site like cattle, grabbing pictures and tacky souvenirs as they passed, muttering about the lack of a coffee shop.

June hid from them. She made her way behind the Parthenon, to the back of the rock. A low wall ran round the perimeter of the Acropolis, and she looked down over it to the ruin of the great Athenian theatre below. A sudden sadness threatened to engulf her. She was upset that her holiday was over, but also at the desolate state of what had once been so great a place, how it had been ravaged by time. She felt so small and insignificant beside the great weight of history around her. Gazing down at the broken, weed-ridden, dusty bowl of the theatre, she felt stupid for almost wanting to cry.

And then, as she watched, with a rasping, grating sound, a blue hut faded into being on the floor of the theatre. At first she thought it must be a magic trick, but that didn't make any sense when there was only her to see it. Even a rehearsal would need technicians and stage managers, checking that the trick worked. June stared, eyes open wide in amazement. A skinny man in a brown suit and trainers emerged from the box. He waved what might have been a mobile phone around, as if trying to get a signal. And then he made his way up the steps of the theatre.

June's brain did cartwheels, trying to make sense of the impossible thing she'd just seen.

Suddenly there were fat, noisy tourists bustling all round her. She waved off their entreaties to take pictures of their group and hurried away back to the entrance gateway. At first she might just been have escaping them, but then she knew exactly where she was headed. Despite the weight of her bag, she took the high steps two at a time, running past the guard, who really was quite cute.

He called out something, might have asked her for a drink, but June could hardly hear him. She ran across the slippery flagstones and then onto the gravel track that ran round the base of the Acropolis, the same path she had climbed that morning.

Soon enough the pathway split off to the right, a sign indicating the *teatro*. By now June was sprinting, grinning, full of excitement for whatever it was she'd just seen. Something strange. Something impossible. Something she had to make sense of.

The path dipped down then rose steeply up. The straps of her rucksack cut into her shoulders, but she ran all the way. She staggered breathless over the summit, looking down on the theatre that had once been able to seat as many as 17,000 Athenian citizens. The blue hut still stood in the horseshoe-shaped space at the bottom, in front of what once would have been the stage.

June made her way quickly down the eroded, uneven steps. And then she stopped, an arm's length from the solid, impossible object, gazing on it in awe. She walked slowly all round the wooden hut, looking for power cables or anything else that might have produced the illusion. Yet she already knew this had been no trick. A sign said, in English, that it was a 'police public call box'. A panel in the door explained that officers and cars responded to all calls. 'Pull to open,' it said. She reached a hand out to do just that, then quickly snatched it away. The panel – the whole hut – trembled with energy. She tentatively reached out her hand again, pressed it flat against the blue painted wood. The vibration felt warm against her skin.

June turned slowly round to gaze back up at the theatre and the high rock of the Acropolis looming above it. There was no sign of the skinny man in the brown suit, but she'd not passed him on the pathway and there was only one other way he could have gone. Quickly but carefully she made her way back up the uneven steps of the theatre, following it further round to her left. Footprints in the dry dust led up to the long, gaping wound in the side of the rock, the sacred caves. June followed the tracks, which had definitely been left by trainers.

The cave felt chilly after the warm air outside. June's forearms prickled with gooseflesh. She made her way into the grotto carefully, not daring to call out, perhaps even a little afraid. Water dripped from long, glistening stalactites. Small, fizzing electric lights cast eerie shadows. And then June could hear voices.

She ventured forward, trying to keep herself concealed behind the rock formations and stalagmites. Up ahead something stank of ozone. The voices were loud and angry but in a language she didn't recognise, made up of clicks and whistles. She crept forward, to find the skinny man struggling in the grip of two blobby grey aliens.

June blinked. Yes, they were definitely aliens. No more than a metre and a half tall, blobby and grey, their flesh glistening with rainbow patterns like on a puddle of oil. Two of them held the tall, skinny man while a third berated him in the clicking, whistling language.

The skinny man struggled but could not get free. He argued back in clicks and whistles but the grey aliens would not be swayed.

The skinny man sighed and shook his head. And glimpsed June lurking in the shadows.

'Bartholomew,' he told the grey alien, now in blokey English. 'You've enough explosives here to take out most of Athens. I just can't let you do that.'

The grey alien seemed to have understood him, and the powerful gravity with which he said it. As it replied in a defensive sequence of clicks, June looked past it to the heap of hefty packages like sandbags. They were stacked around three tall, wide stalagmites, more than the height of a man. Yes, there did seem to be an awful lot of explosives.

'I'm sure you've got the best of reasons,' the skinny man insisted, again with a quick glance in her direction. June realised he was speaking English for her benefit, so she would understand. 'But I'm sorry. I really am. You have to leave right now. Earth's authorities will be here any moment. And you know what humans are like. What a curious bunch they are. Before you can say that you come in peace they'll have cut you open to see how you work.'

And June realised that he didn't just need her to understand. She had to rescue him, too, or Athens would be destroyed. All that wealth of history, the bedrock of the world she knew...

Terrified but determined, June stepped out from her hiding place. The fizzing electric lights behind her cast a huge shadow up ahead. And she suddenly knew what she could do to stop them.

ONE

'Rahrrr!' shouted June as she ran forward. Her voice echoed in the cave and her shadow up ahead might have been twenty metres tall.

The blobby aliens threw their arms into the air and ran off wailing. June moved her hands, her shadow reaching out to grab them.

'Oh no!' called the Doctor after the blobby aliens. 'A human being! Don't leave me!' But he was also laughing.

The aliens hurried behind the explosives they'd stacked up round the three tall stalagmites, and into a silver sphere. June watched them squeeze themselves through the small entrance, which closed like an iris behind them with a high-pitched whirr.

Only the sound didn't come from the silver sphere but from the wand in the skinny man's hand. He lifted his thumb from the control and the blue light on the wand clicked off. The skinny man twirled the wand around his fingers then dropped it back into the inside pocket of his suit.

He wandered over to the silver sphere and knocked on it with his knuckles, as if wanting to be let in. Nothing happened. The skinny man looked up at June and grinned.

'Hello,' he said brightly. 'Don't worry. This is all a dream. You'll wake up any moment.'

'Those were aliens,' said June.

'Uh,' said the skinny man. 'OK. Yeah.'

'Aliens trying to blow up the Acropolis,' said June.

'Yeah,' said the skinny man. 'Good point.' He hurried over to the stack of explosives and began to scrutinise them.

June joined him, determined not to be scared. The man was very tall and gave off waves of confidence, like being up close to a huge stack of explosives was something he did every day. He put on a pair of thick-rimmed glasses and pressed his face up close to them for a good look.

'Need to do this quickly,' he said, 'before it all explodes.'

'Yeah,' June told him. 'That would probably help.'

Each individual fat packet of explosive was connected to the next with a single red wire. The skinny man traced the connections with his index finger, following them round the three stalagmites. Then he stuck his hand in between two packets and began to rummage around.

'Do you know what you're doing?' she asked him, nervous at how roughly he treated the great stack of explosives.

'Sort of,' he said. 'There should be a—' He stopped, his eyes wide, and for a moment June thought they'd both be blown to kingdom come. Then he slowly withdrew his hand from the explosives. In his fingers glinted a tiny silver sphere on the end of a red piece of wire.

'Control box,' he told June. 'Well, not a box. Technically it's a want conduit. But you won't know what one of those is, so let's just call it a control box.' He closed his fingers around the sphere, gripping it in his hand. Then he closed his eyes tight.

When he opened his eyes and his fingers, the small sphere had turned pale blue. The skinny man grinned at June and tucked it back in amongst the explosives.

'Well,' he said, running his fingers through his thick and messy hair. 'That's that taken care of. You just saved the Acropolis. Maybe even all of southern Greece. Well done.'

'But why would aliens want to blow up the Acropolis?' asked June.

'Um,' said the skinny man. He glanced back at the silver sphere in which he'd locked the blobby creatures. 'They said they had a good reason but didn't get round to saying what. I suppose we could ask them but that would mean letting them out of their ship. Oh well. It'll just be one of those things.'

'They were terrified of me,' said June.

'Yes, well, humans are quite funny-looking.'

'They weren't half as scared of you,' she said.

'Yeah,' he said. 'But then I'm obviously not…' He tailed off, glancing up at her. 'I'm obviously not as funny-looking as you.'

'I'm not funny-looking!' she protested.

He looked her up and down, then shrugged, put his glasses away and headed out of the grotto. June seethed for a moment, then realised he might disappear back into his blue hut. She couldn't just let him get away; she needed to know who he was. June ran to catch him up as they emerged into the early-morning sunshine. He turned back to her, a curious look in his eyes. She decided to play it bold, like they were already working together.

'So what do we do now?' she asked.

'We?' said the man, surprised. '*You* forget all about this. Go home. You're…' He hesitated as a thought struck him. June bristled as he looked her up and down again. 'What's your name?' he asked her.

'Uh,' she said, surprised. 'June,' she said.

The skinny man smiled. 'Hello, June. I'm the Doctor.'

She laughed. 'Is that a codename? Do alien hunters all have names like that?'

The Doctor grinned. 'Oh yeah,' he said. 'We're like a league of superheroes. I sometimes wear a cape. Not today, obviously.'

'There's a whole army of you, is there?'

The Doctor tried to hide it, but she saw the change in him, the sadness in his eyes. 'Oh yeah,' he said. 'A whole army.'

June had only just met him but she instinctively reached for his hand. 'It's OK, I'm sort of on my own, too,' she told him.

He nodded, slowly. 'What brings you to Greece in the first place?' he asked her

'How do you know I'm not local?' she said. 'Maybe I can just speak English.'

'Well, yeah,' said the skinny man, like it was obvious. 'But your accent is a dead giveaway. Lived most of your life near… Basingstoke, maybe. But living in Birmingham now. What are you doing out here?'

June swallowed, amazed he could know so much about her just from how she spoke. 'Came to see all this,' she said self-consciously, gesturing down at the ruin of the theatre, the Doctor's weird blue hut on what had once been the stage.

'They performed *Agamemnon* for the very first time on that stage,' said the Doctor. 'Beautiful evening, standing room only. Of course they hadn't invented popcorn. But what a show! Brilliant ending. I won't spoil it for you but they pull this brilliant gag…'

'Yeah, when Cassandra cries out,' June told him. 'I know. I'm doing Classics.'

The skinny man blinked at her. 'Classics?' he said. 'Are they still teaching that?'

'Yes,' said June wearily. She had got a little tired of people asking her why she didn't do a proper subject.

'Brilliant,' said the Doctor. 'I thought it was all vocational courses these days. Not study just for the sake of study. So you're out here to see the real thing.'

'Yeah.'

'Good for you. Better than just looking it up on the internet, isn't it?'

'Or seeing it on TV.'

'I could show you around if you like,' he said. 'As a thank

you for saving the city. We could go to the Benaki Museum, see the sketches by my mate Edward Lear…'

She grinned. 'I've got a train home in an hour,' she said, twisting round to show him her rucksack. 'It's why I've got all my stuff.'

'Oh,' he said. Again she saw the terrible loneliness in him. 'Oh well, can't be helped.'

'Sorry,' she said. 'But I've done the museums. I've done the temples and the forum. And the old city walls at Kerameikos…'

'Not much I can show off to you about, then,' said the Doctor.

'No,' said June. 'Sorry.'

'So what do you make of it?' he said, looking away from her, surveying the ancient theatre. 'I mean, comparing the real place to what you've only read about it?'

June sighed. She'd been trying to answer that very question for herself since she'd first arrived.

'It's difficult to tell,' she said at last. 'You could spend a hundred years here and still not get it. I keep catching glimpses of a whole other world, the colour and texture of the city as it was.' She bit her lip, annoyed that she couldn't put it any better. 'I don't know,' she said. 'They're so far from us now. Despite all the history and archaeology, it's lost behind so many assumptions. How can we ever know what it was like?'

The skinny man nodded, looking down over the ruin of the theatre and his wooden blue hut. Then he looked up at June, gazing at her with deep, dark eyes. June felt her heart beating in her chest.

'You're right,' he said. 'We can't really know without going there.' He gazed down at her, his eyes alive with mischief. 'You know, there might be something I can show off about,' he said.

to e   a   e of

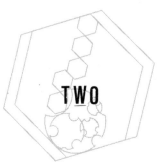

TWO

The TARDIS was bigger on the inside. June quivered with excitement – she was inside a real spaceship! The Doctor rushed round the raised section in the middle of the vast room, attacking the controls. His features were lit by an eerie blue glow from the central column as he twisted and tweaked the levers.

'Right,' he said. 'I've let the authorities know about our aliens and their explosives. Someone will be along soonish.'

'Space police's finest?' said June as she came over to join him. She dumped her rucksack out of the way, under a battered old seat. 'What if the aliens escape before then?'

'I sealed them in,' the Doctor told her.

'Or if someone else sets off the explosives?'

'I used the want conduit. Someone would have to imagine sunflowers and ball bearings to open it.'

'What?' laughed June. 'Why sunflowers and ball bearings?'

'Um,' said the Doctor. 'I like sunflowers and ball bearings. Look, can we go now?'

'Shouldn't I text someone? Let Mum know where I'm going.'

'Go on, then,' said the Doctor. 'But I'll have you back here the very moment you send it. And she won't believe you anyway.' He began to work the controls again, winding a dial and typing coordinates with his long, nimble fingers. 'So. Same spatial coordinates… Just adjust the temporal range… We want somewhere round 480 BC, don't we? When the Parthenon's all spanking new.'

'But nobody will know where I am. What if something happens?'

The Doctor looked up at her. 'I won't let it,' he said. 'I promise. One quick trip, just for a look round. Nothing dangerous. No getting involved in anything.'

A small pink light came on amid the complex controls. The Doctor didn't seem to have seen it.

'Is that important?' said June.

'Probably,' he said, not looking up. 'It's a distress signal somewhere in the area.' He fiddled with some controls and read from the screen in front of him. 'Yeah,' he said. 'Maximum alert, lives in mortal danger, but a thousand years before where we're headed. Someone else's problem…'

June was appalled. 'Who else?' she asked him. 'You said you were on your own.'

'I didn't say that.'

She snorted at him. 'Is there anyone else?'

The Doctor kept his eyes on the controls and didn't answer her.

'Doctor,' she told him. 'Someone's in distress.'

The Doctor looked up at her and she could see his eagerness to answer the call. 'I said we wouldn't get involved in anything,' he told her. And she realised he needed her to take responsibility for the decision.

'It's dangerous, isn't it?' she said.

'Maximum alert,' he repeated. 'Lives in mortal danger.'

'But we should help if we can?'

'I made you a promise,' he said.

'We should help if we can. Do it. Please.'

He grinned at her and began to hammer at the controls. The TARDIS bumped and bucked around them, so June had to reach for the railing. She thought the Doctor had just got them moving at speed, racing to the rescue. But when she looked up his expression was stern.

'That's not right,' he said, eyes fixed on the screen. 'There's a great hole of atemporal mismatch right where we want to be. Off the Kodicek scale.'

'That's bad, is it?'

The Doctor ran his fingers through his hair. 'Well it really shouldn't be there. What happened in Athens in 1500 BC?'

'Did Athens even exist back then?' said June. 'What can this mismatch thing do?'

'Um,' said the Doctor, working the controls, 'it could do worse than all those explosives. So ancient Greece never existed.'

June felt suddenly very cold. 'You've got to stop it.'

'Yeah,' said the Doctor. 'Probably a good idea.' The TARDIS continued to bump and buck under them, the engines groaning under the strain. 'Hang on, we're going to need to pass through it first. Might be a little bit rough.'

June clutched the railing tightly. 'How rough?' she shouted over the noise of the engines.

'A little bit,' said the Doctor.

And then there was an explosion.

The metal grille of the floor pressed hard against June's face. She sat up slowly, her limbs aching. The control room of the TARDIS was dark and smoky, the only light from the steaming central dais of controls. Oxygen masks hung down at head height, like in the safety films on planes. The Doctor stood at the controls, perfectly still and his eyes closed.

'Doctor?' June asked as she got slowly to her feet. She had a hole in the knee of her jeans and felt a sudden twinge of pain when she put weight on her leg.

The Doctor didn't answer. She limped over to him. The screen in front of him showed angry static. Steam hissed from a long fracture in the central column, the light inside cloudy and grey. The steam caught at the back of her throat, a taste of spice and peaches. June hoped it wasn't toxic.

'Doctor,' she said again, scared now by his silence. Again he didn't move. She reached out her hand and prodded him in the arm.

His lips moved.

'What?' she said, leaning in to hear him.

His lips trembled, struggling to form a word.

'Out,' he said.

June stepped back. 'You want to get out?' she asked him. 'But I don't know where we are. We don't know what's out there.'

'Out,' he said again, the pain evident in his voice. 'Get. Me. Out.'

'OK,' she told him. 'Maybe some fresh air will clear your head.' She took his hand, putting her other arm round his waist. He made no response and felt incredibly cold, as if the skinny body inside his suit had been carved from ice. Surely no one could survive being so cold, she thought. But then she'd already come to realise the Doctor wasn't like anyone else.

'I can't carry you,' she told him. 'You're going to have to help me. Can you step back from the controls?'

She hugged him towards her and his legs struggled to respond. He managed one tiny step in her direction.

'Out,' he said again.

'That's right, out,' said June, patiently. 'Come on. Same again. Another small step like the first one.'

With agonising effort he moved his other leg. She hugged him towards her and he took another tiny step. One of the oxygen masks slapped against his face but he didn't seem to notice. His eyes remained closed, his face expressionless, but she could see the desperate effort inside him.

'Have you got a first-aid kit?' she asked him. 'Is there anything I can get you?'

His lips trembled with effort. 'Out,' he said.

There was nothing else she could do but help him.

Slowly – painfully slowly – June led him round the control deck and down the ramp to the door. He could only manage small, shuffling steps and she had to hold on to him to ensure he didn't fall. It took for ever. His knees hardly bent at all.

'You're doing really well,' she told him, breathing hard with the exertion.

Still holding on to him with one hand, June reached for the latch of the door. It opened with a creak. And only then did June fully realise her predicament.

She looked out onto a silvery plain of tall, wild grass, lit by brilliant starlight. They were on a slope, looking down over a long, wide valley, tall rocky outcrops miles off in the distance. A moment ago it had been early morning, now it was dead of night. The air was cool and clean, so clean it made her nose itch. She was somewhere far back in time before the invention of smog. And her only chance of getting home again was this strange man who'd just had some kind of fit.

Terrified now, June stood on the threshold of the TARDIS, not daring to venture any further.

'Out,' said the Doctor behind her.

She turned to face him. His eyes remained closed.

'But we don't know what's out there,' she told him.

He didn't respond. Now she'd taken a breath of the clean air outside, the TARDIS tasted acrid and smoky.

'OK,' she said. 'We're just going to take one step outside.'

She led him through the narrow doorway and out into

the night. A breeze rippled through her clothes, but her shiver came from fear. The ground was hard as iron under her feet, an unforgiving land. She could see nothing but grassland and stars ahead of them, nothing that offered comfort.

The Doctor still had his eyes closed, his whole being closed off from this new world. June stood with him just beyond the door of the TARDIS, feeling utterly alone.

The tall grass shuffled in the breeze – for a moment she thought she saw something moving inside it, but her mind was just playing tricks on her. She scanned the grassy plain, making out occasional outcrops of rock or spindly trees. Off in the distance, starlight twinkled in the calmly moving sea. She turned to see what was behind them. And let out a yelp of surprise.

The hill rose up behind them to a sheer cliff face of rock, the pale stone almost blue in the starlight. The cliff face was raw, untouched by human hand, yet June recognised the crude outline immediately. One day this would be the Acropolis. The TARDIS had arrived exactly where it had set off from, just several thousand years in the past.

A sharp clicking sound in the eerie silence made her turn quickly back round. She ran back to the Doctor, already knowing what it must have been. The Doctor stood where she had left him, perfectly still with his eyes closed. But the door of the TARDIS had shut.

June tried to fight her way in. The metal handle on the door trembled with warmth but the door would not budge.

'You've got a key, haven't you?' she said to the Doctor

as she struggled to get back inside. 'Please tell me you've got a key.'

'Out,' said the Doctor behind her.

June let go of the handle and went to him, taking his hand in hers. 'Please,' she said. 'It isn't safe outside. I don't know when we are but there's nothing out here to help us.'

He didn't respond.

A desperate chill ran through June. 'I can't do this on my own,' she begged him. 'Doctor, I need your help.'

The Doctor's eyes snapped open. For a moment she thought he had come back to her, but his eyes didn't seem to see. She waved a hand in front of him. He didn't even blink.

'I'll have to go through your pockets,' she told him. 'See if you've got the key.'

She reached a hand forward, but just before she reached him he flinched. The sudden movement made her jump.

'Hey,' she said. 'I don't know what else to do.'

'Out,' he said.

'Yes, "out",' she said crossly. 'We're out. I did what you wanted. But now what do we do?'

'Cat,' said the Doctor.

June stared up at him. 'Cat?'

He didn't respond.

'What's "cat" meant to mean?' She dipped her hand into the jacket pocket of his suit. Something behind her purred.

Ever so slowly, June withdrew her hand and then turned slowly round.

It took her a moment to see the cats, hidden in the tall grass.

There were three of them, each about two metres long with muscular bodies and long, muscular limbs. Only one of them had a mane; it was the two females who dared to pad forward out of the grass towards her.

'Cats,' said the Doctor again, simply.

'No,' June told him. 'Lions.'

THREE

June stared back at the lions, utterly terrified. The three lions regarded the Doctor and June but didn't come any further forward. They seemed wary of them, and the long shadows cast by the light from the TARDIS. Which gave June an idea.

'Rahrrr!' she shouted, running towards the lions while waving her arms above her head. The lions took a few steps backwards, more out of surprise than fear. But, unlike the blobby aliens from before, they then stood their ground. They let June run up as close as she dared, regarding her with amusement.

She stopped just in front of the two females. The lead lioness sniffed at her curiously. Its fur shone white in the starlight, its muscles taut with power. June looked in awe at the long, sharp fangs, the claws like enormous razor blades. The lions were perfectly evolved as predators and

June stood right in their path. Yet the lead female then hung its cat-like face on one side like a kitten wanting to play. Its yellow eyes glittered with mischief.

'Hello, moggy,' June told it kindly. 'Who's a big, fluffy cat, then?' She blinked her eyes slowly at it, remembering something off the telly about that being how cats smiled.

The lioness blinked its own eyes back at her, as if in understanding. It rocked back slightly on its back legs and she thought it might be sitting down, accepting her, wanting her to tickle its belly.

Then it pounced.

'Help!' cried June as she fell back from the outstretched claws, the teeth, the whole huge creature launching itself at her. In her fear, her legs wouldn't respond. She tumbled into the hard ground, eyes open wide on the lioness barrelling through the air towards her, the great silhouette blacking out brilliant stars…

And a slender shape darted between her and the lioness. It twisted in and up, pressing itself into the nook of the lioness's shoulder. The lioness was spun deftly over onto its back. It crashed down into the earth just beside June, the impact jolting right through her body.

She and the lioness exchanged startled looks. Then the lioness looked up at the silhouette of the man that had thrown it over his shoulder. And, with a kitten-like mew, it slunk off to rejoin its friends.

June scrambled up onto her feet, behind the Doctor. He stood perfectly still, majestic in front of the three lions.

'In your own time, then!' she told him, but he didn't respond. His eyes were open but she saw the same lack of expression on his face. He'd snapped out of his coma to save her, but now, just a moment later, she had lost him once again. 'Oh, come on,' she said, slapping her hand against his shoulder. 'This isn't fair!'

The lioness he'd thrown now skulked behind the other two lions. June almost felt sorry for it. But its friends weren't so easily put off. The male stepped forward and roared at the Doctor, filling the still night with its challenge. It was so loud it made June's ears ring. Yet the Doctor didn't seem to notice. The male shifted back on its haunches, ready to pounce on him. There was nothing June could do.

And then it and the two lionesses just turned round and fled. In a moment they were lost in the long grass, completely invisible within it. What might have been the movement of three lions could just as well have been the breeze.

Only then did June hear the low rumbling behind them. She turned to see a horse racing towards her, dragging a simple, two-wheeled chariot behind it. A short, slender woman in a gleaming, egg-shaped helmet gripped the reins, a second woman behind her brandished a bow and arrow.

The horse snorted as the chariot came to a halt beside June and the Doctor. June held up her hands, showing she carried no weapons. She smiled her sweetest smile but felt her heart turning over. The woman with the bow leapt nimbly out of the chariot and came over, the bow pointing right at June. She wore a simple tunic. Long dark hair ran down her back in plaits, tightly coiled ringlets framed a pretty face.

'I thought we were cat food!' June told her, eager to make friends.

The woman with the bow couldn't have been more than one and a half metres tall, and gazed up at June warily. Thick black mascara emphasised almond-shaped eyes. June realised with a shock that these slender, capable women couldn't be out of their teens. And that they wouldn't understand her, even if she spoke to them in Greek.

'You'll come with us,' said the woman with the bow – in English.

'What?' said June, taken aback. 'Please,' she told the two warrior women. 'My friend is sick.'

'You'll come with us,' repeated the woman with the bow. 'Or you will die.'

'Oh,' said June. 'Well, if you put it like that...'

The chariot sped across the rocky ground and June had nothing but the Doctor to hold on to. He lay curled up, like a giant child, his top half in her lap. She cradled him, not knowing what else to do.

June had no idea how the two tough warrior women stayed on their feet as they raced along. It was hard enough just sitting in the chariot, her legs hanging over the back. The chariot was a low, oblong box, the frame made from slender branches of wood, the panels just pale, stringy leather, springy under their weight. June supposed it worked like suspension, but they didn't half bounce around. She could feel the vibration through her teeth and limbs.

She glanced up at the warrior women piloting the

thing. They wore long swords on their belts, the dark metal scuffed and tarnished with use. Their bare legs were tanned and scarred. June felt puny sat with them on the chariot. She wondered what they had planned for her and the Doctor. Were they prisoners, or slaves, or worse?

The two warrior women leant back as they clasped the reins, but otherwise had nothing to hold on to. They just had to balance expertly, a bit like they were water-skiing. It would only take a slight mistake to throw them out onto the rocky ground. No seatbelts, thought June and gripped the Doctor a little tighter.

They rode on, round the base of the high rock which would one day be the Acropolis. Cold air seethed past them as they went. June considered escaping. She could easily hurl herself from the back of the chariot and just keep running into the night. By the time the women noticed and had turned the chariot round, she might have found somewhere to hide. But she wouldn't be able to take the Doctor with her, not in his current state. And without him she would never get into the TARDIS, she would never get back home. Her fate was bound to him. She could merely sit on the back of the chariot and wait to see where they ended up.

But they were not going far. Up ahead, between the main bulk of the Acropolis and a smaller outcrop of rock, stood a wooden wall. It looked crude but strong enough to keep out wild animals. And, as the chariot drew closer, June could see it had been built quite recently.

A door creaked open in the wall and the chariot slowed up to trot easily through. They entered a small open area surrounded by new, wooden stables. Horses snorted and shuffled around in the shadows. As the warrior women brought their own horse to a stop, human faces peered from the dark openings. When June looked round to stare back at them, the faces melted back into the darkness.

The warrior women leapt out of the chariot and began to tend the panting horse. They murmured encouragement and wiped the sweat from its flanks. One of the women began to uncouple the chariot from the ties around the horse's neck and body. The other, the woman with the bow, came over to June and the Doctor.

'I will take him,' she said, and before June could protest she had scooped the Doctor up in her arms and put him over her shoulder. His long skinny body hung like a dead weight. The warrior woman carried him away.

'Hey!' June called after her. She scrambled off the back of the chariot, legs all pins and needles from the ride. 'I need him!' she called as she followed warrior woman up a flight of simple wooden steps leading to the great rock. The wood smelt new, freshly hewn, and shifted slightly underfoot. It looked like the planks were only held together by rope. She hoped it wouldn't collapse underneath her. Then she emerged onto the top of the rock.

She started in amazement. The Acropolis she knew so well now looked so different, devoid of its ancient monuments. Instead of the great temple to Athene, a few wooden dwellings clustered round each other, a tiny community on the long expanse of rock.

A single stone building stood to one side, its roof the same shape as a beehive. Smoke coiled from the chimney at the top. The warrior woman carried the Doctor towards it.

'Let me help with him,' called June as she hurried to catch up. The warrior woman bowed her head to step inside. June reached the doorway and stopped. She could feel the warmth from inside on her bare, cold face. But there was also a strange, spicy stink emanating from the darkness. It made June's nose tingle. But she couldn't let them take the Doctor from her. She stepped into the darkness.

It took her eyes a moment to adjust, and then to make sense of what she was actually seeing. Through the low porch she emerged into a simple, square room with a large space for a fire at its centre. Embers glowed warm and red in the fire, the only light in the room. It made for a solemn, religious atmosphere, a place of peace and contemplation. Scented smoke curled from three-legged pots placed at regular intervals round the room.

The warrior woman stood on the far side of the fire, where she lay the Doctor down on the ground. Shoes squeaking on the stuccoed floor of coloured zigzags, June hurried round to reach her. The low light made it difficult to tell what the colours might have been, but June guessed red and gold. Everything seemed red and gold in here. Firelight glittered in the polished ceiling and from the golden clothes of the people painted on the walls.

By the time June reached her, the warrior woman was on her knees beside the Doctor's body, her head bowed low in prayer. A bearded man in a striped tunic squatted down on the other side of the Doctor and ran his fingers over his face. He wore thick gold rings on each of his fingers and gold bangles on his wrists. June could see he must be important, so she knelt down beside the warrior woman and tried to look respectful.

The man continued to work, placing his hands over the Doctor's eyes and intoning some kind of prayer. He was a wiry, athletic man who had seen a fair few battles. A savage, long-healed scar cut down his forehead, missed his eye then continued down his cheek and under his thick, dark beard. Long gold earrings dangled from his ears and he wore some kind of gold tiara. He looked up at June with beautiful, dark eyes.

'You have no magic of your own?' he asked.

'I don't have anything,' said June, her voice wavering with awe. 'I think he just needs rest.'

'Then he shall have rest,' said the man with satisfaction. 'I command it.' He smiled, his teeth in pretty good order so many thousands of years before the invention of toothpaste. June smiled back, eager to win him over.

'Thank you,' she said. 'He's my only chance of getting home.'

The man nodded. 'You are from the future,' he said.

June stared at him. 'How did you know?'

The man laughed. 'Your clothes. Your size. Your expectations.' He nodded at the warrior woman. 'We will eat,' he told her. The warrior woman hurried out.

The man stood, and took June by the hand, helping her to her feet. She towered over him. Some men she'd met didn't like that, but he didn't seem to mind.

'My name is Actaeus,' he said, bowing to her. 'My people and I are at your service. Your friend seems comfortable.

His breathing is regular. His hearts are beating steadily. Perhaps he just needs to sleep.'

'Thank you,' said June. She didn't ask what he meant by the Doctor having hearts, plural – perhaps it was a belief thing. 'I'm June. Forgive me, but you said "your people". Are you the king?'

Actaeus smiled sadly. 'I was the king of a great province once. Had a home in a town of stone buildings. But an earthquake tore it down. And then my sons were taken…' He tailed off, a terrible look in his eyes.

'I'm sorry,' said June. Actaeus looked up at her, surprised. For a moment, June thought that she had said the wrong thing, that it wasn't done to pity a king. But then he smiled.

'Thank you,' he said. 'Please. Won't you sit by the fire?'

She perched on the wide bricks running round the fireside, a warm and homely spot. The Doctor lay perfectly still on the stuccoed floor, just as if he were asleep. Actaeus gathered some logs from a heap and tossed them onto the fire, then came to sit next to her. The embers crackled and spat at the dry logs and bright yellow flame erupted round them. June felt the heat pressing through her clothes, the muscles in her neck and shoulders starting to unwind. Perhaps the past wasn't so bad.

Actaeus looked about to say something. But then there was a movement from the far side of the fire. June turned to see two young women run in, carrying trays. They were beautiful, dressed in tight bodices and long flounced skirts. In fact, they moved with such girlish elegance and grace that June didn't recognise them at first. But these were the two warrior women who had captured her and the Doctor.

'My daughters,' Actaeus told June. 'Aglauros and Pandrosos.'

'How do you do,' said June to the two princesses. They smiled at her, though she saw something cold and dead in the eyes of Aglauros, the scars of some terrible calamity. Aglauros glanced quickly away, then looked back with a forced smile on her face, defiance in her eyes. Eager not to offend, June looked away, admiring their exquisite jewellery, delicately hewn pieces of gold and lapis lazuli in the shapes of butterflies and flowers.

'I've never seen gold worked so beautifully,' she told them, though she had seen something similar behind glass in a museum.

The princesses – if that was what they were – grinned and giggled back at her. They behaved like children, nothing like the warriors she'd seen before. But she also realised she had misunderstood them. They hadn't threatened her, they had offered her sanctuary. If they'd left her and the Doctor out in the open she would have been eaten by the lions. 'Come with us,' they'd said, 'or die.' They had meant it kindly.

'Your daughters saved our lives,' she told the king. 'They saved us from three lions.'

She'd expected the king to be pleased but his expression darkened. 'They must learn to hunt the lions,' he said. 'It is all I can do to protect them.'

'The lions attack you?' June asked.

Actaeus glanced away from her, over at the paintings

glittering on the wall. 'My daughters will be ready,' he said. He clearly didn't want to be drawn on this, so June let it be. With the Doctor unconscious, she needed these people on her side.

Aglauros, the older of the two princesses, knelt down before June with a clay basin and jug. Again, June could see the girl struggling with some inner torture, but thought better of asking about it outright. Maybe if they were alone together sometime, she could have a quiet word.

They took turns to wash their hands in the clay basin. Aglauros only put her right hand forward, keeping her left to one side. It took June a moment to realise why: just as with the Greeks and Romans, these people ate only with their right hands. Until people invented toilet paper, their left hands were used for something else. June copied Aglauros, washing her right hand. When she was done, Aglauros held out the cloth.

Pandrosos came forward with shallow clay bowls of what looked like stew, chunks of meat in an oily sauce. Following Aglauros' example, June dipped her fingers into the hot, sticky sauce and extracted a cube of meat. It squished between her fingers, drooling oil down her hand. She popped it into her mouth and chewed. Her eyes widened in delight and she made appreciative noises at Pandrosos.

They didn't talk as they ate, which was good because it took concentration. June couldn't help getting oily sauce down her wrists and chin, but the king and princesses didn't seem to be doing much better. She found herself grinning as she ate. Being messy was fun.

When they had finished, Aglauros came forward with the basin and jug so they could wash their fingers. Actaeus burped loudly, making his daughters laugh. Then he offered his hand to June and helped her to her feet. The princesses began to gather up the bowls.

'Can I help?' June asked them. The princesses looked surprised.

Actaeus laughed. 'You are an honoured guest,' he said. 'And a worse fate awaits you.' June froze. But Actaeus only smiled at her. 'The history of our people is painted on the walls.'

'He bores everyone with the paintings,' said Aglauros, like her dad was getting out the family photos.

'Not everyone,' Actaeus chided. 'Only honoured guests.'

'Then I'd be honoured,' June told him, which made Aglauros laugh. Actaeus led her over to the walls. He didn't say anything at first. Instead, he stood back, letting June look over the pictures, making sense of them herself.

The scenes, painted right onto the plaster, showed slender warriors in the same egg-shaped helmets Aglauros had been wearing on the chariot. They marched in formation and fought in a war and perhaps one scene showed a wedding. As well as the soldiers there were women and children, and scenes of strange, mythic creatures.

June tried to match the creatures to the Greek legends she knew – things that might have been griffins, or the giant bird of prey called a Roc. But she couldn't place the enormous, bald monsters with claws the length of a man and staring, wide black eyes. They emerged from a building with slender fins and engines, clearly some kind of spacecraft.

'Aliens,' she said, in horror. 'They're aliens!'

'They are our masters,' said Actaeus, loyally. But June could see he didn't like it, his whole body bristled as he said what was expected. 'They feed us and help us, and in return they only ask for a small payment. That we pay them willingly.'

'But who are they?'

Actaeus looked confused. 'They are our masters,' he said. 'They are called Slitheen.'

'They're not your masters,' said a voice from behind them. They turned in surprise to find the Doctor sitting up. Light glittered in his eyes, alert and intelligent. His expression was deadly serious.

'I've met them before,' he said. 'And trust me, you don't owe them anything.'

FOUR

'**D**octor, you're alive!' said June, running over and hugging him. He patted her back rather awkwardly and after a moment she withdrew.

'Sorry if I scared you,' he said, scooping up some of the stew in his right hand. 'But you seem to have done OK. Where are we? Who are the people in all the bling?' He stuffed the meat into his mouth and his eyes opened wide as he chewed.

June glanced back at the king and two princesses. 'This is King Actaeus and his daughters, Aglauros and Pandrosos. They rescued us. From lions.'

'Thank you,' nodded the Doctor. 'This lamb is really good. Lentils. And some coriander?' Pandrosos nodded eagerly. 'We're very flattered.'

Pandrosos bowed. 'We only had a little left,' she said.

'But it's just what I needed,' said the Doctor. 'Something

to latch on to. Focus the synapses and… Those other things like synapses. It'll come back to me.' He ran his tongue round his teeth and then grinned. 'You know,' he said to June, 'some people show their love by cooking. I love people like that.' He took another great handful of food.

'I'm glad you're feeling better,' said Actaeus, coming forward to sit with them. It struck June as odd that a king would sit on the floor. But he seemed keen to welcome them into his home as equals.

'I just needed a bit of a sleep, I think,' said the Doctor. 'I don't know what June has told you…'

'You're from the future,' said Actaeus.

The Doctor turned on her crossly. 'You told him that?'

'No!' she protested. 'Really, he worked it out himself.'

The Doctor considered. 'Oh, well, all right then.' He turned to Actaeus. 'You've met people from the future before.'

'Our masters,' said Actaeus, nodding his head at the frescos of aliens. 'We are meant to show you hospitality.'

The Doctor nodded. 'Treating strangers well is just good manners,' he said. 'I hope you're not forced against your will.'

Actaeus smiled. 'You and June have simpler needs than some,' he said gently.

The Doctor put his bowl down. 'Tell me what's happening here,' he said.

Actaeus narrowed his eyes. June could see his quick mind picking over the Doctor's words. 'You don't already know?' he said.

'I want to hear how you see it yourself.'

Again Actaeus considered. 'This is some kind of test of loyalty?'

'Actaeus,' said the Doctor. 'I can't help you if you won't tell me. Tell me as much as you want.'

'You said we couldn't get involved,' said June.

'The Slitheen are here,' he said. 'I have to know what they're up to. First time I met them they were going to blow up the world. And then there was Margaret, who wanted to blow up Cardiff. And then… Look, it doesn't matter. What are they doing back in time, at this critical moment in history?'

'They can't change anything, though, can they?' said June. 'I mean, it's already happened. I'm proof of it. I exist.'

The Doctor looked her up and down, then prodded her arm with his oily finger. 'Yes you are,' he said. 'Let's keep it that way, shall we?'

Just for an instant June pictured her home, her parents, her friends at university, even her ex-boyfriend, Bruno. All of them, everything she'd ever known, thousands of years of human history. And it could all vanish in a blink of an eye. Where would that leave her? Would she vanish as well?

'What can we do?' she asked the Doctor in a quiet voice.

He looked up at Actaeus. 'How long have the Slitheen been here?'

'Since before my father was born,' said Actaeus. He took a deep breath and began. 'They came from the sky and they saw we were hungry. They gave us food. They saved us from ourselves.'

The Doctor groaned. 'Oh, it's not going to be the official version, is it?'

'It's our history,' said Actaeus. 'It is all we have.'

'Don't be rude,' June chided. 'You asked to hear it.'

'I'm sorry,' said the Doctor. 'Please, go on.'

'They have fed us, they have helped us to find peace. And in return they ask only for a small payment.'

'I thought there would be a price,' said the Doctor. 'And what do they take from you?'

Actaeus faltered. Aglauros came forward to sit with him, and he put an arm around her. Both had such terrible looks on their faces.

'You don't have to tell us,' said June. 'Doctor, please.'

The Doctor's face was stern. 'No,' he said. 'You don't have to tell me. But I know the Slitheen of old. I know what they do. And I've beaten them more than once.'

Actaeus sighed. 'We give them what is asked for,' he said. 'We are loyal.'

'What do they take?' insisted the Doctor.

But Actaeus glanced at Aglauros and would not say anything more.

'I had two brothers,' said Pandrosos, coming forward to stand behind the king. 'They were our future. They were good boys. Though they teased me when I was small.'

'And I had to box their ears on more than one occasion,' smiled Actaeus. 'But then Aglauros was going to have a baby. She became my daughter. We were happy! A grandson for the king. An heir for the kingdom.'

'And then the order came,' said Aglauros, her eyes suddenly dark hollows.

'It was not an order,' said the king. 'It was a request.'

'But you couldn't say no,' said the Doctor.

'There are stories sung of those who say no,' Actaeus told him. 'But we don't even know their names.'

'They're punished?' asked June appalled.

'They're wiped from history,' said the Doctor. 'Isn't that right?'

'Isn't it better that a man surrenders the lives of his sons than those of all of his people?'

'Did you think so?' asked the Doctor.

'I told myself it was the right thing to do. And they were young. Keen to take the challenge. They wanted to go.'

'What happened to them?' asked June, though she didn't really want to hear it.

Actaeus shrugged. 'The request said they would compete for the glory of my kingdom. They went. We have heard nothing more. And then the earthquake came and destroyed my kingdom anyway. And…' He tailed off, his voice breaking.

'And I lost the child,' said Aglauros. June wanted to reach out to her, to hold her, to show some kind of sympathy. But Aglauros sat stiffly apart from them all, an awful deadness in her eyes.

'Some think it was a sign,' said Actaeus at length.

'That you made the wrong choice?' asked June.

The king looked up at her with surprise and anger, as if she had just slapped him. 'That my sons had failed,' he said. 'That they would not be coming home. The town fell. We hid in the ruins and were prey to wild animals. So those of us left now shelter on this rock. The animals can't climb the walls of our stockade. And other tribes keep away from this place anyway.'

'Why?' said June. 'It's a great position. You can see for miles. Isn't it a valuable spot?'

'Our masters come here, sometimes,' said Actaeus.

'They come here?' asked the Doctor. 'Why?'

'Perhaps it is the view,' Actaeus smiled bitterly.

'We're on the Acropolis,' June told the Doctor. 'Or what will be the Acropolis.'

'Ah,' said the Doctor. 'And they come in groups, do they? The Slitheen plus brightly dressed parties of other creatures?'

'Yes,' said the king. 'They come to point at us and cast the magic that paints our image in the air. There is a ritual. The Slitheen forecast the future and the other creatures laugh.'

'And then they head off to other historical sights,' said the Doctor.

'I do not know,' said the king. 'But they never stay for long. That is why we gambled we could stay here.'

'They're running a package tour!' June realised. 'See Athens before they build it.' She turned to the Doctor. 'Can they do that?'

The Doctor sat back, finishing his meal and thinking. 'Who's going to stop them? This period of your history is full of tales of gods and monsters. Perhaps the Slitheen have always been here. Perhaps they're meant to be.'

'You think this is fate?' asked Actaeus. And something

about him had changed. He sat forward, alert, and his smile had gone.

'It's just a theory,' said the Doctor. 'But there's something else, isn't there?' The king hesitated and glanced at his two daughters.

'You don't have to tell us,' said June kindly. But she hoped that would only make him tell them.

'We have had another request,' said Actaeus. 'And this time they ask for my daughters.'

To June's horror, the Doctor would not offer his help. He didn't say no, but he didn't say yes either. June wanted to argue with him. Of course they should get involved. The princesses were off to their deaths! She realised why the king had sent them out to fight with lions. He had hoped to train them as warriors so they might stand some chance.

But instead, Actaeus changed the subject. He and the Doctor wiled away an hour discussing the different needs of herding sheep. June couldn't relax. She watched the two princesses, who sat politely listening to their father. In their eyes she could see their torment, their fear. But they were too well brought up to argue. At one point Aglauros glanced at her, and they shared a pained and desperate look. But then Aglauros looked away again, all meek smiles for her father.

June turned to the Doctor. And for all he gabbled on about how he'd once had to rescue a ram from a crocodile with only a wooden spoon, she could see the conflict in his eyes. No matter how long she watched him, he would not meet her gaze.

Then at last, without anyone having to say it, the evening had come to an end. Aglauros and Pandrosos went over to a wooden box at the edge of the room and from it produced woollen blankets. These they laid around the central fire.

'Well, thanks for tea,' said the Doctor to Actaeus. 'You've been very kind. June and me should get back to the TARDIS.' He turned to June. 'Do you know where it is?'

'Sort of where we left from,' she said. 'South side of the rock.'

The Doctor grinned. 'Really? I'm not always good at those tricky manoeuvres. And in the middle of a crash…'

'You can't leave the compound at this time of night,' said Actaeus. 'There are lions out there.'

'Yeah,' said the Doctor, 'but I've got this thing with cats. Didn't to begin with, but we're on a wavelength now.'

'Doctor,' said Actaeus. 'You can't leave the compound. I'm sorry, I need your help.'

The Doctor stood tall, towering above him. 'You can't force me,' he said. He spoke firmly, with menace. June was almost scared of him.

The king smiled. 'And I would not want to. But in the morning, let me make my plea again. Then, if you are not persuaded, you can go in peace. You have my word.'

The Doctor considered, glancing at June. 'All right,' he said. 'But don't expect me to change my mind.'

June grinned at him, but again the Doctor would not meet her eye.

FIVE

The stuccoed floor was hard underneath her, even when June doubled up the blankets. But it wasn't just the floor that kept her awake. She watched the embers of the fire. The princesses slept beside their father, the Doctor next to June. No one else seemed troubled by the worries worming through her mind.

How could they leave the king to give up his daughters? She understood that the Doctor didn't want to rock the boat, that the aliens and their strange requests might have always been a part of history. But surely if she and the Doctor could help, they were obliged to try. After all, aliens had stopped being masters to humans at some point in history. Why couldn't that happen now?

But then, what could they really do to stop them? These aliens must have a sizeable operation going on. What difference could two people make?

She turned over, trying to make herself comfortable. And found the Doctor watching her. He smiled then glanced over at the king and his daughters. The king was snoring.

The Doctor put a finger to his lips and then untangled himself from his blankets. He had not taken off his trainers, and she realised he'd never intended to stay. She reached for her shoes, lying beside her bed, but he stopped her from putting them on. Of course, she thought, she'd make less noise on the stuccoed floor if she escaped in bare feet.

They made for the door on tip toes. June could hear her own heart hammering in her chest. She glanced back at the fire where the king and the princesses lay. And Pandrosos was sat up, watching them. There was a terrible look of disappointment in her eyes. She reached a hand forward to wake the king. And then she decided not to. Pandrosos lay back down, turning away from the Doctor and June, pretending to be asleep.

Feeling wretched, June followed the Doctor out into the biting cold night. It took her a moment to get her shoes back on, the cold air whipping at her clothes. The Doctor again put his finger to his lips, then led her down the creaking wooden steps to the stockade. A man in a long cloak stood guard on the gate. His egg-shaped helmet seemed to have long teeth sewn all over it and for a moment June thought they might have been his. But they were too long for a human and there were too many of them to have come from one person. She guessed they'd belonged to some animals.

'Wotcher,' said the Doctor as he ambled over to the

guard. He rummaged in his inside pocket and withdrew a leather wallet. 'His majesty has given us a secret mission, but this says all you need to know.' He opened the wallet, showing a blank white page.

The guard on the gate grinned widely, showing many missing teeth. 'I don't actually read,' he said.

'Oh,' said the Doctor, snapping the wallet shut. 'That's a bit of a problem.'

'But I'm sure it must be all right,' said the man. 'Only an idiot would want to go out this time of night. You know there are lions out there?'

'Yes, we know about the lions,' said the Doctor. 'But orders are orders. You know what his majesty's like.'

The man immediately stood more erectly. 'I won't speak ill of the king,' he said.

'No, of course,' said the Doctor. 'But you know what he's been through. Best just let us do what he says.'

The man opened the gate and the Doctor took June's hand to lead her through. 'Rather you than me,' said the guard as he closed the gate after them. 'See ya.'

June tried to speak to him as they hurried across the rocky ground but again the Doctor put his finger to his lips. Perhaps their voices would travel up the sheer slopes of the high rock to the community asleep on top of it, she thought. But it seemed more likely the Doctor just wanted to avoid the argument.

She held his hand tight in hers and struggled to keep up with his long, nimble strides. Another reason not to start arguing now was that their voices might attract lions.

But too late. The night air was torn by a rumbling growl, and a large male lion padded towards them. He didn't seem to think they posed much threat – he approached them rather casually. June felt almost insulted.

'Hello, kitty,' said the Doctor soothingly.

'I tried that,' June told him. 'It doesn't work.'

'No?' said the Doctor, as if June were being mean to think such nasty things of the poor pussy cat. He fished in the inside pocket of his suit. 'But I've got a little treat for kitty in here.'

'I don't think he's a reader, either,' said June. But the Doctor withdrew the short magic wand she'd seen him use in the future. He pressed the button and the tip of the wand buzzed with electric blue light. The Doctor raised the wand and aimed it right between the lion's glinting eyes.

June waited for the wand to zap the lion with laser beams or lightning. But instead the lion stopped in its tracks and just lowered its head forward, so the beam of blue light tickled over its scalp. The Doctor waved his wrist around, moving the spot of light up onto the lion's ears and back again. To June's amazement, the lion started purring. Warm, contented breathing filled the silent night.

'Naw,' said the Doctor, not getting any closer. 'Who's a big fluffy cat?'

June took a step closer to the lion, ready to tickle its ears. But the Doctor grabbed her hand. 'Best not,' he said. 'Just in case.'

He switched off the beam of light and the lion growled with frustration. The Doctor switched on the beam again, and the lion flopped over on its side, letting the Doctor tickle its tummy with the light. It waggled its legs in such a silly, kittenish way that June burst out laughing.

'Come on, then,' said the Doctor. 'Which way's the TARDIS?'

June led him on and the lion padded after them, keeping a respectful distance. It felt more like a loyal dog than any kind of cat now. And, June hoped, with this one tagging along with them, no other lion would try its luck.

Eventually they could see the distinctive shape of the TARDIS, stood slightly at an angle on the bare rock. The light on the roof and in the high windows of the door glared bright in the starlit darkness. Immediately June felt safe. They hurried on, the lion bounding after them, enjoying this strange game.

As they reached the doors, the Doctor handed his wand to June, showing her the button to press. 'Go careful,' he told her. 'We don't want him too excited.'

June buzzed the blue light around the lion's forehead and then over the back of its neck. The lion rolled over on the ground, purring with delight. June laughed out loud again at this, and the lion turned to look at her sternly. This was no laughing matter.

While she continued to play, the Doctor fished in his pocket for the key. The door of the TARDIS creaked open, light pouring out from within.

'Come on, then,' he said, and June hurried after him into the time ship. The lion mewled and scratched at the closed door.

'Right,' said the Doctor, hurrying to the central column of controls. 'You're going to tell me we *have* to get involved.

That we can't stand by and just let the king give up his daughters.'

'Are you going to tell me that we can't?' said June, joining him as he worked the complex systems. 'That we don't want to change anything that's already happened?'

'Er, yeah,' he said. 'I think you're gonna be good at this.' Then his head whipped back to the instruments before him. He put on his thick-rimmed pair of glasses to read the screen as information scrolled across it.

'Well,' he said, 'the TARDIS is feeling better. Needed a sleep just like I did. Lost its bearings when we went through that area of atemporal mismatch. Probably because, by definition, it doesn't have any bearings. Capiche?'

'No,' said June. 'I have no idea what that meant.'

'Me neither. Never mind. If we leave we might have to pass through that time storm again, which isn't exactly ideal. And if we stay we might not be able to resist bothering the Slitheen.'

'You think the Slitheen have always been here? That they're meant to be?'

'You're the classicist,' he said. 'You know the stories of the ancient Greeks.'

'But they don't speak of monsters called Slitheen,' she said.

'Well, they might not have known the names. Or they got lost in all the retellings. You ever played Chinese Whispers? That's how all of human history works until someone thinks to write it down. And then writings are lost or translated badly…'

'So we leave them to it,' said June sadly. 'And the

king loses both his daughters. As well as his sons and grandson.'

'Maybe,' said the Doctor, busy with the controls. Then he stopped, just gazing at the screen. He began to work the instruments again. A map appeared on the screen. June recognised the snaggled coast of the Greek mainland and some of the nearer islands. Peculiar writing scrolled across the map, then a pattern of red dots. One marked the site of the Acropolis, another the island of Aegina. And several red spots speckled the island of Crete.

'What do the red spots mean?' asked June.

'Some sort of spatial something,' said the Doctor as he worked. 'Time bending a bit like a localised black hole. Probably a transmat or some other warp system for jumping from place to place.'

'So they can tour the main highlights of ancient Greece in the same afternoon.'

'Yeah,' said the Doctor. 'And make sure the people living here all behave. Hmm.' He adjusted controls and more information scrolled down the screen. 'But there's nothing else. No cities. There aren't even any large towns. Human beings should be much more advanced than this now...' He twiddled some more. 'I can't even see any farms. How are they feeding themselves?'

'Actaeus said they were hungry and the aliens had fed them.'

'Yeah,' said the Doctor, running his long fingers through his hair. 'But that's only a short-term solution. You people forget how to grow your own food and the whole species is finished.' He leant forward to work the controls and the map zoomed out to show Europe and the top half of Africa. Red dots speckled various places of interest.

'There's Stonehenge and the Pyramids,' said the Doctor. 'But they're already old. There's nothing from this time. Nothing being lived in or used. The only place that's got any large building is…' He tailed off. 'Oh, yeah,' he said. 'Of course.'

'What?' asked June. But she couldn't read the peculiar language. 'How come I can understand Actaeus and his daughters, but I can't read what's on the screen.'

'Never mind,' said the Doctor. 'The Slitheen have gone too far. Oh, if they hadn't been greedy we could have turned a blind eye. But the operation's too big now. It's having too much of an impact. At this rate they're going to squeeze the human race out of existence.'

'Yeah,' said June, 'because if only they'd killed less people it would be OK.'

'*Fewer* people,' the Doctor sighed. 'And not OK, no.' He stepped back from the controls. 'Right,' he said. 'Time to go.'

'Where?' said June. 'I mean, can't we just go straight to wherever we're going? Isn't that what having a time ship is for?'

'Yeah,' said the Doctor. 'But there's that atemporal mismatch hanging round us like a bad smell. And anyway, turning up at Slitheen HQ in this thing is going to get their attention. They'll be looking out for disturbances in time. So Plan B.'

He hurried down the ramp to the doors of the TARDIS. 'Coming?' he asked.

She took the magic wand from him, ready to quiet the lion. 'But I don't know where we're going,' she said.

They snuck back into the stone building on the top of the Acropolis. June's shoes slapped on the coloured, stuccoed floor. They tiptoed to the blankets, still lying strewn where they'd left them. The Doctor grinned up at June as they both sat back down. She grinned back. No one need know they had ever been away.

But she looked up at the sleeping figure of Actaeus and his daughters. And Actaeus gazed back at her.

'Oh,' she said.

'Shh,' whispered the Doctor. 'You'll wake—' He turned to see the king and grinned a silly grin. 'Oh, sorry,' he said. 'We didn't mean to wake you.'

The king folded his arms. 'You left us,' he said. 'You stole off in the night like thieves.'

'Yeah,' said June. 'But we came back. Didn't we?'

'And what have you decided?'

'Oh, you'll like this,' said the Doctor. 'Your daughters don't need to go anywhere.'

'And then our masters will destroy us,' said the king.

'Nah,' said the Doctor. 'Because you're going to send them something better in their place. You're sending me and June.'

SIX

The sun beat down hard on them as they raced across the rocky ground. June held on tight to the Doctor, arms wrapped around him. He leant back, laughing and whooping as he drove the chariot. If she hadn't been so scared, she'd have hit him.

The lining of her boars' tusk helmet felt rough against her hair and ears. Apparently all warriors wore them. Otherwise, the Doctor and June were off to compete in just the clothes they'd turned up in – June in old jeans and a T-shirt, the Doctor in his slim suit. Aglauros had doubted whether she'd find any local clothes big enough to fit them anyway.

They had strapped a curved oblong shield made of hairy ox hide into one side of the chariot and also a few paltry foodstuffs in case they wanted to stop for lunch. The Doctor had declined any weapons, to the princesses' amazement. How, they said, could he go off to fight without anything to fight with? Pandrosos had tried to press a dagger on June when the Doctor wasn't looking, but June turned it down. She wanted to believe in what the Doctor had said – that they could sort this all out without anyone getting hurt.

The Doctor drove fast yet skilfully. June felt sure she was being bounced around less than she'd been the previous night. Or perhaps it helped to be standing up, so that your legs took all the vibration. She clung on to the Doctor, knowing that if he made a mistake or lost his balance they'd both be in serious trouble. There were no straps to put your feet into, no crossbar at the front of the chariot to press against with your knees. The only way you didn't fall out was by leaning back, your own weight balanced against the horse's.

Moving her head, she caught the breeze as it whistled around the Doctor. The air tasted fresh and clean, thousands of years before car engines and industry. But there was something else, a familiar, nose-itching tang. She eased her grip on the Doctor a bit to glance around.

They were riding through a shallow valley, over low-cut grass. The grass looked dry and sandy coloured, with regular dollops of dung. Across the valley, sheep and goats chewed nonchalantly, ignoring the chariot as it whizzed past. A shepherd waved at them cheerily, but June didn't dare let go of the Doctor to wave back.

'You know where we're headed?' shouted the Doctor.

'To see these Slitheen people,' she said into his back.

'Well, yeah,' said the Doctor. 'But where we're headed

first. We're heading down through what will one day be Athenian suburbs to the port of Piraeus.'

Again, June leant back from him to glance around. Yes, she could more or less make out the contours of the land, the gradual slope down which they were racing. She had caught the tube to the port at Piraeus just ten days ago. By high-speed ferry, you could spend a day on the nearby island of Aegina and be back in Athens for the evening.

A thought struck her. 'Doctor,' she said. 'If we're going by water, it's going to take us ages.'

'Won't be more than a week,' he called back.

'I can't be gone for a week!'

'It's all right,' he said. 'I'll still get you home the moment that we left. Nobody will notice.'

'But I will! I'll be a whole week older. My birthday will be all out of synch.'

'Well, what do you want me to do? Turn back and take you home now?'

June didn't say anything. She bit her lip in irritation.

'Look,' said the Doctor. 'This is going to be fun. You don't get seasick do you?'

'Yes,' said June.

'Oh,' said the Doctor. 'Well, apart from that, it's going to be fun.'

There was nothing even resembling a port at what would one day be Piraeus. The Doctor brought the chariot to a halt in front of a long, sandy beach. A few other people in twos and threes watched each other warily. They carried spears and long swords and all kinds of other weapons. One pair had the same curved, oblong shields as the Doctor, while most had shields that looked like a stretched figure eight.

'We don't want any trouble,' the Doctor told June quietly as he helped her down from the chariot. Her legs were numb with exhaustion. Riding a chariot had proved to be quite a workout. She started to unhook the horse. It snorted and shook one of its legs, then cantered off down the beach, neighing happily. She could feel the other competitors watching her. And two stocky, bearded men in metal armour came over to the Doctor.

'Who are you?' one asked.

'Oh, no one really,' he said, admiring their armour. 'A whole bronze suit,' he cooed. 'You must be rich and important. So you don't want to be slumming it with the likes of me. I'll get out of your way.'

He bowed and stepped away from the stocky men. But one of them grabbed him by the shoulder.

'Doctor!' cried June, running forward. The other stocky man stepped forward to intercept her, withdrawing a long sword from his cloak. June skidded to a halt in the sand in front of him, just out of reach of the sword. Other competitors came closer, eager to see the fight.

'Ow!' said the Doctor to the stocky man holding him by the shoulder. 'Watch out. Not all of us are wearing armour!'

'You talk too much,' said the stocky man. 'The warriors of Berbati are more about action than words.'

'Is that where you're from?' asked the Doctor, wincing under the man's grip. 'Berbati's lovely this time of year. Ow. Look, would you mind letting me go?'

'Say you're sorry,' June told him. 'Please.'

'I'm sorry,' said the Doctor. 'Can't we all be friends? I guess we're all here for the same reason.'

'Yeah,' said the stocky man. 'To fight. And you don't have anything to fight with. So might as well kill you now.'

Before June could cry out, the stocky man had reached for a blunt cudgel hanging from his belt. He swung it high above his head, brought it crashing down on the Doctor. But the Doctor twisted, caught the man's wrist in his hand and held it, the cudgel just clear of the top of his head.

The stocky man gaped. He could not move his hand.

'I won't fight you,' the Doctor told him. 'Unless you force me to. And trust me, you don't want that.' He tightened his grip on the man's wrist. The stocky man yelped in surprise. It might even have been funny, were it not for the terrible look in the Doctor's eye. 'Do you?' he said.

'No,' said the stocky man.

'Good,' said the Doctor, letting him go and smiling. 'We're better working together. Best of the best from all across Greece. Working against the Slitheen.'

The stocky man regarded the Doctor coolly. June saw the other groups of soldiers glancing at each other. And the man with the sword in front of her, the stocky man's friend, heading for the Doctor.

'Watch out!' cried June. The other man in armour was now running at the Doctor, his sword held aloft.

'No,' shouted the stocky man, stepping past the Doctor to intercept his friend. But the sword was already coming down. The stocky man twisted, slapping his blunt cudgel against the edge of the sword. It hit with an ear-splitting crack, and the man with the sword spun round, off balance, smacking into the man with the cudgel. Both collapsed in a heap just in front of the Doctor.

'I mean it,' the Doctor told them pleasantly. 'The Slitheen have got us all fighting each other because we're easier to control that way. It's classic divide and conquer. But we can take them on.'

The stocky man lay tangled up with his friend on the sand. 'How?' he asked the Doctor.

The Doctor extended his hand to the man. 'You stick with me,' he said. The stocky man glanced at the other soldiers all around them. He lay prone, defenceless. But he'd been offered a chance. June grinned as he reached up and took the Doctor's hand.

They built a barbecue on the beach while they waited to be collected. June wasn't the only woman, but all were warriors of the first rank. They came from the main towns of Greece – Kokla, Mycenae, Tiryns – and all had the same stories to tell. Earthquakes had ravaged their kingdoms. The Slitheen masters provided their food. And in return they asked only for a small token payment. Every community had to send warriors to compete for glory.

The Doctor organised the cooking, casually asking questions about the earthquakes and the Slitheen. June helped, building the fire, preparing the food, chatting to the other competitors. Most people had their own small provisions, but the stocky man, Alyon, organised fishing rods and a group of volunteers. Soon they were cooking long, silvery fish in the hot ashes of the fire. More pairs of competitors arrived as the afternoon wore on. There were maybe as many as seventy of them by the time the sun had set.

They served up, and a portly, red-nosed fellow produced an amphora of wine. He also led the singing once they'd eaten. Soldiers sang of their homes, their loved ones, the stories of their people. They told stories in which they were the heroes, in which they brought glory home. June and the Doctor joined in with the choruses. Then they wanted to hear June's story, to hear what the future was like. They all seemed quite familiar with the idea of time travel, but had never met a human being from the future before.

She tried to wriggle out of it but that just made them more insistent. They laughed and applauded and called her name. Eventually she gave in.

'I'm nothing special,' she told them. The soldiers heckled and booed, dismissing this idea. 'Well, all right,' said June, 'I'm great. But my life is pretty ordinary. A nice mum and dad, nice friends, a nice life. A bit of trouble with boys.' Alyon wolf-whistled and the soldiers laughed. June found herself blushing. 'I'm OK,' she said. 'Just nothing to sing stories about.'

Alyon tutted. 'You are the most important one here,' he told her and the other competitors. 'Because you give us hope. That one day our lives will be better. That the Slitheen will be gone and there will be no more struggle.'

June smiled sadly. 'I wish I could show you,' she said. 'It's not perfect, but it's all right.'

'There's always struggle,' said the Doctor. 'The struggle to do what's right. The struggle to provide for a family, to learn, to make things better. It wouldn't be life if it wasn't hard work. But things do get better. So long as you lot can work together.'

'What are you proposing?' asked Alyon.

The Doctor stared into the fire, saying nothing. June nudged him with her elbow. 'Go on,' she said. 'We have to do this.'

'But the Slitheen can wipe out their people if they resist,' he said.

'And if they don't resist, all humanity is wiped out.'

'We don't know that. Perhaps this is how it always was.'

She snorted. 'Doctor, does it *feel* right? The ruins of kingdoms at the beck and call of aliens? We're no better than slaves.'

The Doctor gazed into the fire. And then he got to his feet. The firelight glinted orange off his bony features, sparkling in his eyes. 'All right,' he told the assembled, eager soldiers. 'This is what I think we should do...'

The eight boats arrived before dawn. They were long, flat-bottomed cargo boats with huge, square sails and nobody was sailing them. In eerie silence the boats moved at speed across the water, to line themselves up on the beach.

'It's impossible,' said June.

'It's just magic,' said Alyon. He and the other competitors began to load their possessions onto the boats. Each boat could take about ten competitors and their luggage. The passengers sat on the boxes of cargo.

'I don't like this,' said the Doctor as he helped June into one of the boats. 'I don't like no one being in control.'

June didn't like it either – the boats seemed so small and vulnerable. She remembered the last time she'd been seasick. The sickness had three awful stages. First you thought you were dying, then you *knew* you were dying, then you really *wished* you were dying.

The Doctor must have seen the look in her eyes. 'You could stay here,' he told her.

'We'll be fine,' she told him, even more horrified at the thought of him leaving her behind. 'These things run on magic. They're automatic, like a monorail or something.' The Doctor didn't seem any happier.

When the boats were all loaded, they simply glided backwards out onto the water, turned and headed out to sea. They moved so smoothly that June could close her eyes and believe they were perfectly still. The other competitors marvelled at this ingenuity, but the Doctor sulked at one side.

'It's not really sailing, is it?' he said.

Soon the rocky peaks of Greece were no longer visible behind them, and the sea stretched to the horizon. The sun rose ahead of them, painting the sky and water all the shades of orange and pink. June sat back to enjoy the show, enjoying herself. But she noticed the competitors on the other boats whispering nervously to one another.

'They're having second thoughts about what you said,' she told the Doctor.

He watched the soldiers, then followed their nervous glances to the sky ahead of them. 'No,' he said. 'It's something else.'

The sky ahead of them had turned a beautiful crimson.

'I love a sunrise,' said June. 'You watch it from Delphi and you can see what the ancients meant. The chariot of day chasing away the night.'

But the Doctor looked serious. 'Red sky in the morning,' he muttered. 'Ask any shepherd. That's really not good news.'

He hurried to the back of the boat, pushing past a portly bloke who was looking rather poorly. The Doctor pressed and poked at the back of the boat, but could find no workings.

'What is it?' asked June.

'There's going to be a storm,' he told her. 'I want to check these things will cope.'

June gazed up at the red sky again. Yes, it did look a little angry. And there were dark clouds on the horizon. She felt a moment of terror.

The Doctor produced his magic wand and began buzzing at the boat's mast and moorings. It had little effect.

'Don't worry,' he said. 'I'll fix it. Go and find someone to talk to. Take your mind off it.'

June's stomach gurgled with fear as she left the Doctor to his work. She sat unsteadily down beside the portly bloke, who looked wan and ill. 'Feeling seasick?' she asked him.

He grinned. 'Hardly. It's a hangover. Should have watered down the wine. My own silly fault.'

'I'm June,' she told him, extending her hand.

'Deukalion,' he said, taking her hand and kissing it. His dark beard felt rough against her fingers. But his eyes were bright and young – he couldn't have been much older than her.

'You're not a soldier,' she said.

'No,' he admitted. 'My fighting days are long past. But the kingdom needed someone to send and they thought it might as well be me.'

'What did you do?' she asked.

'I didn't do anything!' he protested, then he clutched his head in both hands. 'Ow,' he said. 'I am never drinking again.'

'What did you do?' she asked him again.

'I dared to suggest a king was wrong on a matter of principle,' he said.

'A matter of principle,' said June sceptically.

'Yes,' said Deukalion. 'The queen can snog whoever she likes on her birthday. That's one of those things about queens.'

'And you were one of the people she snogged.'

'I might have been,' said Deukalion. 'And then the masters said they wanted people to compete for his glory. And I got volunteered.'

June laughed. 'I bet you did.' Deukalion beamed at her. And behind him the sky was black.

'Doctor!' she cried as the boat lurched sickeningly underneath them. The sea that had been so perfectly calm now churned with dark power. A great wave clattered over the side of the boat, soaking those sat up by the prow. It began to patter with rain, fat globules smacking hard against June's skin.

'Everybody keep down,' said the Doctor, struggling to

the front of the boat, brandishing his magic wand. Just the way he took command made June feel a hundred times less terrified. 'We've got to—'

But his words were lost to the awful roar of the rain now lashing down. The boat smacked hard against another huge wave and tipped almost at a right angle. Then the wave had passed and they slapped down hard onto the water. The force knocked the Doctor from his feet, sent him slithering back towards where June and Deukalion were kneeling.

'Ow,' said the Doctor. He grinned. 'This is more like it. A proper sailing trip!'

Despite her terror, June grinned back at him. His features were lit up by electric blue lightning, the crash of thunder right on top of it. They turned quickly round to see the mast of one of the other boats sparking into flame. Soldiers screamed, and one fell into the water. June thought she saw Alyon on that boat. The lightning flashed again and the sail was ablaze.

Their own boat suddenly lifted and dropped sickeningly as the waves crashed against them. June clung on to the Doctor, lungs raw where she'd been screaming.

'It's all right!' he yelled, barely audible over the storm. 'We're going to be all right!'

And then a wave smashed so hard into them that the boat was turned right over. June fell through the air and then through cold, dark water.

SEVEN

The cold sea embraced June, held her tight. It weighed upon her, tried to stop her thrashing her arms and legs. She fought against it, no idea which way was up or down. Water clogged her nostrils. Sound rumbled dumbly all around her.

She struggled to remain calm, looking into the dark, murky depths for anything that could help her. Cargo floated past her head: a sword, a helmet, a sandal. She kicked in the other direction, making for the surface.

June burst from the water, wheezing in the air. Rain lashed her face and a great wave grabbed her, lifting her high into the angry night. Thunder rumbled and men cried out. As the wave peaked and began to fall, she looked down on the wreckage of boats and people. Not one boat remained upright.

The competitors could not swim. She saw one man

struggling in the water, his arms wrapped round a torn-off piece of wood. June kicked her legs and swam to him. Her progress was better after she'd yanked off her shoes and socks, swimming in bare feet. But when she reached the man he tried to fight her off, instinctively protecting the wood that kept him floating.

'It's all right!' she shouted to him over the noise of the storm. 'I can swim. I just want to help.'

The man turned to her. It was Deukalion. His eyes were wide with fear. He tried to reply to her but couldn't get the words out.

'It's OK,' she told him. 'It's going to be OK. We just have to find the Doctor.'

Another wave rolled underneath them, and Deukalion let out a low moan. June reached for him, grabbed his shoulder, then tucked her arm gently around his neck. She had learnt lifesaving at school and remembered the manoeuvres. Deukalion tried to fight her off, but the water had sapped all his energy. He surrendered to her, nestling the back of his head in her shoulder.

'Try and lie out flat,' she said, gently in his ear. She trod water, keeping them afloat and stable. Deukalion's breath became more regular.

'We're...' he wheezed. 'We're going to die.'

'I'm not going to let that happen,' she said. She looked all round, searching for anything that might help. The sea churned around them, lightning flashing in the dark. And the light picked out two faces in the water. June whooped and waved with her free hand. The second time the Doctor saw her and waved back. He too had someone in tow.

June waggled her legs as best she could and carried Deukalion slowly over towards the Doctor. It seemed to take for ever, the waves working against them. June had to swim backwards, dragging Deukalion after her, so she couldn't see where she was going. She kept being slapped in the face by water rebounding off Deukalion, and he did nothing to help her. She wanted to let him go just to wipe the hair back from her face. But she resisted the temptation screaming inside her. Painfully slowly, they made their way through the water.

'OK,' shouted the Doctor. 'You're going to have to reach his hand.' June couldn't see where he was, but he sounded close. Something clonked down hard on her head, stunning her for a moment. She relaxed her grip on Deukalion, sank down into the water. The wetness on her face and eyes brought her to her senses. She struggled back up, grabbing Deukalion, who was struggling from her grip.

'Sorry, sorry,' she heard the Doctor calling. And then Deukalion let out a cheer. He stopped struggling, and she ducked round, moving his head to her other shoulder so she could see what he had done. He held his arm aloft, out of the water, linking hands with another man also lying in the water. The other man must have clonked her on the head as he reached for Deukalion. June glimpsed a familiar spiky quiff on the far side of the man's shoulder.

'Doctor!' called June, her voice high and raw.

'Hello!' he said cheerily, ducking his head round that of the man he'd saved so he could see her more clearly. He wore a ridiculous, wide grin, his eyes open wide. 'Knew you'd be around here somewhere.'

'You don't lose me that easy,' she told him. 'What are we going to do?'

The Doctor glanced all round. 'We're passing through the storm, I think. Just got to keep together. Calm waters coming up.'

June swallowed, the seawater full of salt. 'I can't see anyone else,' she said.

The Doctor's smile faltered. 'No,' he said. 'If we can find something for you lot to cling on to, I can go for a look…'

'There isn't anything,' she said.

The Doctor held her gaze, an awful expression on his face. 'No,' he said. 'No, there's only us.'

They rode out the storm together. The Doctor asked them all questions, keeping them awake. June felt comfortable in the water, as comfortable as sitting by the fire with Actaeus, the same warm contentment flooding through her. She felt the numb ache in her muscles and knew she need only relax her grip of Deukalion to slip away into the water's embrace. It would be easy, and she so wanted to sleep…

'Oi, June, it's your turn,' called the Doctor. 'First kiss.'

'Yeah,' said Deukalion, his head nestling in her shoulder. 'I had to tell you mine.'

'All right, all right,' said June. 'First proper kiss was with a boy called Jonathan. At a bus stop, when we were fourteen.'

'Hah!' laughed Vik, the man the Doctor had rescued. 'I got *married* at fourteen.'

'That late?' asked the Doctor.

'My second wife,' said Vik.

'I had two wives,' mused Deukalion. 'But both at the same time.'

'How did that work out?' asked June.

'Oh, it was good,' said Deukalion. 'Until they found out about each other.'

They drifted on, chatting about nothing. June could almost have enjoyed it. The rain died down to a drizzle and the waves slowly levelled out. June told them about Bruno and Melissa, the boyfriend and best mate she had run away from. Vik offered to hunt them down for her. Deukalion said that, if she wanted, June could be his third wife.

'I think we're coming out of it,' said the Doctor.

June looked up. Dark cloud gave way to bright blue sky. The sun pressed warm against her face.

'This isn't so bad,' she said.

'Um,' said Deukalion. 'We're still in the middle of the sea.'

June glanced round. The water reached to the horizon all round them. But when she turned back to the Doctor he wore a stupid grin.

'Oh, brilliant,' he said. He nodded his head, indicating the far side of where Vik lay in the water.

June kicked, bobbing out of the water high enough to see over him and Deukalion. To where the two square-sailed boats awaited them.

June hauled herself into the first boat, to find two people already lying on its floor. She recognised the woman from the barbecue the night before. She had a great speaking voice, like a proper actress, and had told a story about a clever owl. Her name was Herse. The man introduced himself as Polos.

Vik and Deukalion clambered up into the boat. June watched the Doctor climb into the boat just across from them. He hunted around, waving his magic wand at various bits of it, then kicked the central mast in frustration. It only hurt his foot. He muttered something angrily, then saw June watching him and grinned at her with embarrassment. Deciding the other boat offered them nothing, he dived neatly overboard to join June and the others.

For a long time they just lay there in the boat, soaking and exhausted under the sun, spreading their clothes out to dry. But the Doctor lay looking out to sea, his eyes searching for any other movement, for any other survivors.

'We could go back,' June said to him, after she'd recovered a bit. She found it difficult to move, her limbs aching from all that time in the water. Yet the horror of all the people they'd lost weighed down on her.

'How?' said the Doctor dejectedly. 'This boat's sitting perfectly still on the water, ignoring the current underneath it. I could get out and kick and it wouldn't make any difference.'

'But you've got your magic wand.'

The Doctor withdrew the device from his pocket. 'It's a sonic screwdriver,' he said. 'But the boat is deadlock sealed. They don't want us wandering off.'

'So we just sit here?' said June.

'Until they decide they've waited long enough for survivors.'

'But all those people!' said June. She thought of Alyon, and all those who'd sung stories. All of them were gone.

'Think of it this way,' said the Doctor. 'We're way back in your past, so these people had been dead for centuries even before you were born. Like watching early films or something. You see the people, you hear them speak, but they're already gone.'

June watched Deukalion, Vik, Herse and Polos. She couldn't think of them like that. They were alive here and now. She shared their exhaustion and pain. The Doctor saw her expression and smiled sadly.

'No,' he said, putting an arm around her. 'It doesn't work like that, does it? I'm sorry.'

'You read history,' she said quietly. 'You read about a time when the average life span was 25 to 40. Or you read the statistics for children dying young. And you think people must have been different back then. That they must have got used to it.'

'You saw Aglauros,' said the Doctor. 'You never get used to it. Each death wears you down. You keep pressing on. Struggling to survive, to build something better. Whatever the odds against you. Indomitable.'

June didn't feel very indomitable. She lay back in his arms, watching their other shipmates sprawled out under the sun. There were only six of them left now to face the dreaded Slitheen.

EIGHT

When June awoke, the two boats were gliding swiftly over the water. Sore and exhausted, she joined the Doctor at the back, looking out over the barely discernible wake.

'Feeling better?' he asked.

'Not really,' she told him hoarsely. 'Told you I got seasick.'

'Seems smooth now,' he said, eyes on the calm water.

'Yeah,' she agreed. 'But it was before. That storm came out of nowhere.'

'That's what I was thinking,' said the Doctor. 'And then there are all these earthquakes.'

'It happens round here,' she said. 'All over Greece and Turkey. Even in our time.'

The Doctor nodded. 'Mmm,' he said. But he didn't seem convinced.

Maybe it hadn't been an accident. June shuddered at the thought – why would anyone inflict something like that on them? She left the Doctor to his dark thoughts.

June's clothes were pretty much dry, if stiff from drying in the sun. Her money and student ID card had mushed in her wallet. It shouldn't matter, she knew, but it hurt her. These ruined bits of paper were all the proof she had of where she came from, of her real life.

Determined not to cry, she joined the others, watching over the curled prow of the ship for wherever they were heading. They comforted each other, telling more of the stories they'd shared round the camp fire – who they were, where they came from, the things that were important. Deukalion hugged his sides, looking pale and sick. Herse had her arm round Polos, the man who had rescued her. He came from a town on the coast of Boeotia, he told them, and learnt to swim as a child.

The sun passed above them and behind to the left. June couldn't remember which direction that meant they were heading in. But at last a dark line appeared on the horizon. June called the Doctor over, and in the seconds it took him to join them, they were looking at a long coastline of rocks and trees. Their exhaustion gave way to excitement.

'Where is this?' asked June, but the Doctor didn't answer. He pointed at the long grey buildings at the top of one high cliff.

'It's a stone building,' said Polos, amazed. 'Look at the size of it. Like the old stories! They must be safe from the earthquakes out here.'

The Doctor said nothing, his eyes narrowed as he

watched. The boats came to rest on the thin crescent of beach at the foot of the high cliff. They tumbled out onto the hot, fine sand, soft between June's bare toes. She collapsed forward, lying face down, just glad to touch dry land. The Doctor sat down beside her.

'No one's here to meet us,' he said.

June looked up and around. The beach filled the shallow inlet in the cliff, but they were cut off by deep water from which poked jagged rock. There didn't seem to be any way off the beach but for the boats they'd just arrived in. A line of green on the cliff wall showed how far the tide came in to the beach. It reached well above their heads.

'Oh no,' she said as she sat up. 'We're not out of this yet, are we?'

'I think they like to keep us guessing,' said the Doctor.

Deukalion, Vik, Polos and Herse wandered round the crescent of sand, stretching their legs and exploring. But they could see no way off the beach, either. They came back to the Doctor and June, plumping down in the sand.

'We're playing someone else's game,' said the Doctor. 'We wait for their next move. But remember, we're in this together.'

They sat waiting all afternoon. The tide washed up towards them, each time coming an inch closer. They moved back up the beach as the sea claimed it, until their backs were up against the cliff. The tide lapped around their ankles, pulling at them as it fell back. Each time it returned it had a little more strength.

'Just keep together,' said the Doctor. 'We can get through this.'

'I can't swim,' said Deukalion. He glanced round at June. 'Can we do what you did before?'

'We'll be fine,' June told him. 'Just do what the Doctor tells you.'

The sea splashed against her shin, then sucked around the back of her knee. Even when the tide withdrew, water still covered her ankles.

'Um,' said June. 'Doctor. Have you got any ideas?'

The Doctor was gazing out to sea, a strange smile on his face. 'You know,' he said, 'I don't think that storm was meant to happen.'

June blinked at him. 'What?' she said.

'It doesn't make sense. I mean, what was it meant to achieve?'

Water lapped against June's thigh. 'Doctor, now isn't exactly the time.'

'But doesn't it bother you?' he said. 'Because if the storm hadn't happened, what would we be doing?'

'Well,' said June. 'We'd still have ended up here. Only there'd be lots more of us.'

A terrible thought struck her.

'There'd be too many of us.'

'Exactly,' grinned the Doctor.

'Seventy people,' said Deukalion. 'All fighting against the tide.'

'All fighting each other, more like,' said Vik.

'You'd all want to be up against the cliff,' said the Doctor.

'But there's only room for a few of us,' said June. 'So it would get nasty.'

'It *could* get nasty,' said the Doctor. 'Maybe you'd work together.'

'You think so?' asked June.

'It's a nice idea,' said the Doctor. 'But you've all been told you're competing with each other. Perhaps this is the first round.'

'Great,' said Deukalion. 'I mean, that's really clever what you've worked out. But the tide is up to my waist now!'

'Oh yeah,' said the Doctor. 'It has to look like you're in real danger. You're meant to be fighting for your life.'

'It'll be OK,' said June, taking Deukalion's hand. He squeezed her fingers tightly, watching the water rise up round his middle. 'If it comes up to your shoulders, you just float on it again. We'll be fine.'

The water came up to her armpits, and then no further. It lapped and splashed around her arms, and Deukalion started laughing.

'We're OK,' he said. 'We're OK.' He leant over to kiss June on the forehead. She ducked away before he could follow that with a kiss on the lips.

'So now what?' she asked the Doctor.

'They'll come for the ones who are left,' he said. 'We'll be on to the next round.'

Stars began to peek from the darkening sky, and a cold wind ruffled the surface of the water. June shivered, but Deukalion squeezed her hand. Vik, Polos and Herse huddled close together, keeping warm. 'We could always do that too,' Deukalion said to June.

'I'm fine,' she told him.

He looked crestfallen. She assumed he'd pulled the same

puppy-dog face when his wives met one another.

'Ah,' said the Doctor. 'Here we go.' Behind them, higher than the level of the water, the pale cliff face rippled inwards. They looked up into a dark opening.

The Doctor reached his hands up to it and hauled himself from the water. He disappeared into the darkness for a moment, checking it was safe. Then he hurried back, a wide grin on his face. He reached down to help June out of the water. 'Come on, then,' he said. 'You're not going to believe this.'

A huge, tall cave had been carved out of the rock. June and the others stood on a narrow stone platform, the gap out to the sea just behind them. The platform was about a metre wide, running round one edge of a deep pool of water, in which floated an enormous ship.

The hull was more than sixty metres long, the dark wood curving elegantly up out of the water to the deck. Three huge masts reached up almost to the ceiling of the cave, the vast sails tethered by a complex system of ropes. It was a majestic, beautiful vessel – but thousands of years out of place.

'It's the *Cutty Sark*!' said the Doctor. 'Or a very good copy.'

'But why's it here?' asked June.

'They probably use it for pleasure trips,' said the Doctor. 'Bit more comfortable than those boats.'

'How do they get it out of the cave?' asked Polos.

The Doctor looked round the cave. 'There must be some controls somewhere.'

'But it shouldn't be here,' June insisted.

'What?' said the Doctor. 'A Victorian tea clipper in the late Bronze Age?'

'Yeah,' said June. 'It doesn't make sense.'

'Oh, it makes sense,' said the Doctor. 'It just shows the Slitheen don't give a stuff about history. Come on.'

He led them along the platform round the side of the huge ship. They made their way down the dark corridor at the back of the platform, water clattering noisily from their sopping clothes. June worried her jeans might shrink after two long soaks in cold water, but there was little she could do about it now. The Doctor led them, June close behind him, Vik, Polos and Herse. Deukalion was at the end, muttering quietly to himself – but loudly enough for the others to hear – that they were all going to die.

But they walked for an hour without incident. A warm breeze pressed against their faces, slowly drying their hair and clothes.

The corridor led them slowly upwards, and then they reached a flight of stone steps. Light glittered down on them from somewhere high above, so they were just able to make out the edges of the steps. They were weary after all the time in the water, and every step was exhausting. But slowly they climbed up towards the light.

The Doctor stopped them within sight of the top landing. Noise echoed from the lit passageway ahead, the noise of many people.

'We can't go back,' whispered June.

'No,' said the Doctor. 'But just remember…'

'We're all in this together,' they chorused.

'Um, yeah,' said the Doctor, awkwardly. 'I suppose that proves it.'

Deukalion sniffed. 'Until you want to do your own thing,' he said.

'You'll see,' said the Doctor. 'Everyone ready?' They nodded. 'OK,' he said. 'Let's go.'

They emerged into a wide, square courtyard larger than a football pitch. People in all kinds of costumes were busy training in the centre. June gaped at them, trying to make sense of it. There were people in spacesuits, people dressed as Vikings, people in the leather uniforms of Samurai. Two Roman centurions duelled with wooden swords. Women in heavy, old-fashioned police uniforms practised karate moves, dancing around in bare feet.

June turned to the Doctor, hoping he'd explain. But he was gaping too.

'They're from all through time,' said June. 'Brought here to compete.'

'It looks like it, doesn't it?' said the Doctor. 'But they're not. Real Vikings didn't have horns on their helmets.'

'And the police should be wearing boots,' said June.

'Yes, they should.' He and June looked round. The courtyard was bordered by a high gantry, from which the sport could be watched in safety. June's heart leapt into her mouth.

Terrifying creatures pressed against the railings. Some had long, scarlet tentacles, others glistened with dark spikes. One fat creature belched clouds of dark blue gas.

'Aliens,' she said, in awe. Yes, she'd known there were

aliens here, but actually to *see* them… It was incredible.

'Tourists,' the Doctor corrected her. She glanced at him, then back at the throng of strange creatures. And she almost had to laugh. The aliens nattered noisily and took pictures, exactly like the brash tourists she'd seen hulking round the Parthenon. Even in outer space, tourists were still tourists.

A man dressed in a suit of armour clanked over to the Doctor and June and the others. 'Quick,' he said. 'You'd best start training. Give them something to look at. They'll make bets on how you do.'

'Right,' said the Doctor. 'You lot get going. Make it look good. I need them to be watching you.'

Vik, Herse and Polos hurried into the centre of the courtyard and began a number of well-practised fight moves. June assumed they had spent months training to compete in this contest. They looked professional and a little scary.

'Aren't you going?' she asked Deukalion.

'No,' he said. 'I'm sticking with you. Just like you said.'

'It might get nasty,' the Doctor warned him.

'But June's going with you,' said Deukalion.

'He does have a point,' said June.

'All right,' said the Doctor. 'Welcome aboard. There's just a few rules…'

'Look,' said the man in the suit of armour. 'Whatever you're doing, get on with it. The masters don't like us just talking.'

'Right,' said the Doctor, chastened. 'Thanks.' He led June and Deukalion across the courtyard, through the duels and play-fights. A pretty girl in a khaki camouflage ball gown did an awesome high kick as they passed. Deukalion veered towards her. June grabbed his arm and ushered him on.

They ducked into the dark cloister under the alien-stuffed balcony. Blood-red columns held up the balcony, looking oddly upside down because they were thicker at the top than they were at their bases. The Doctor whipped his sonic screwdriver from his suit pocket and buzzed it on the lock of the door. With a click, the door swung open and they passed quickly through.

'Right,' said the Doctor. 'We just need to find where the Slitheen are hiding,' he said.

'Oh, really?' gurgled a high, childish voice. Three long claws slashed out of the darkness, round the Doctor's neck, lifting him off the floor. The creature stepped forward, slapping the Doctor's body against the wall. June gaped up at it in horror: two and a half metres of green flesh, wet and wobbling, naked but for a bracelet round one wrist. Its long, scaly neck curved over at the top, like an upright prawn, its huge head leering down at the Doctor, struggling in the grasp of its claws. The bloated green face was like some warped, mutated baby with huge, jet-black eyes. It smiled, showing razor-sharp teeth.

'I'd say,' it giggled at the Doctor, choking in its grip, 'that you've found us.'

NINE

Deukalion ran for the door but it had closed behind them. He squealed as he tried to force it open. June watched the Doctor hanging from the Slitheen's long talons, his legs wheeling in the air. She watched the Slitheen grinning at its prey and tried to think of something she could do. The Slitheen towered over her, its green muscles glistening and taut.

'Wait,' she begged it. 'Please!' She tried to think what would appeal to the huge alien creature. What would it care about? The Slitheen giggled gleefully as it closed its grip around the Doctor's neck. 'If you don't let him go,' June said sternly, 'he'll give you a bad review.'

The Slitheen twisted its long neck to look down at her. Huge black eyes blinked expressively.

'He'll do what?' it slurred. Thick spittle drooled from its lips. The Slitheen had breath like old baked beans.

Behind them, unable to get the door open, Deukalion continued to squeal.

'A *damning* review,' said June, willing herself not to flinch. The Slitheen blinked at her again. Then it twisted its head to look back up at the Doctor.

'Is he famous?' it asked suspiciously.

'Me?' said the Doctor, straining in the grip of the enormous talons. 'No, not famous exactly. Have to travel incognito. You know how it is. But I've got some identification if you could just see your way to letting me down…'

Carefully, the Slitheen placed the Doctor back down on the ground, but kept its claws loosely clasped around his neck. The Doctor fished in his inside pocket and produced his battered leather wallet. The blank page inside dazzled the Slitheen, who jumped back a couple of steps.

'Oh my word!' it gurgled, throwing its claws into the air. 'A gazillion apologies! We weren't informed you'd be coming!'

The Doctor flapped the wallet closed and stuffed it back in his pocket. Then he straightened his tie, looking serious and in charge. 'Well,' he said hoarsely, 'that's sort of the point. I'm meant to be invisible.'

'Oh yes, of course,' the Slitheen bowed obsequiously. 'I never saw you, honestly.'

'Well, you've seen me now,' he said. 'Hello. I'm the Doctor. Travel critic for the *Mutter's Spiral Herald*. This is my assistant June and our local Passepartout, Deukalion.'

The Slitheen curtsied at June. 'Charmed,' it gurgled. 'I'm Cosmato Fel Fotch Hangle-Wang Slitheen.'

'How do you do,' said June.

'Help,' said Deukalion, pressed up against the door.

'My friends call me Cosmo,' said the Slitheen quietly. 'You can be my friends if you want.'

June raised an eyebrow at the Doctor. 'Would that be appropriate?' she asked him archly.

Cosmo took another step back. 'I only meant to be friendly!'

'Oh,' said the Doctor grinning. 'I think we can all be friends, can't we? You'll have to forgive my assistant. Right one for the rule book. Gives me an earful just for parking on an up-quark!'

The Slitheen bobbed its head between them, trying to work out which of them it wanted to side with. 'Well,' it murmured. 'Rules are there for a reason.' It had clearly decided June was the one to fear.

'Yeah,' said the Doctor appreciatively. 'I suppose that's right. I'm glad I met you, Cosmo. You're a pretty shrewd observer.'

'It is one of my skills,' admitted Cosmo modestly.

'Well,' said the Doctor. 'We normally do this on the quiet. Nose round on our own. But since you've been sharp-eyed enough to spot us, I guess we might as well have the tour.'

Cosmo nodded. 'Oh yes,' he said. 'I'd be delighted. What would you like to see?'

The Doctor's eyes twinkled. 'Absolutely everything.'

June found it hard to make sense of the layout. Instead of main hallways and corridors, the citadel – as Cosmo called it – had some 1,300 rooms connected by various small corridors. Rooms sprung from other rooms, so they might as well have been traipsing through a maze for all she could get her bearings. Cosmo proudly showed them the theatre, the vast storerooms of clay vases, and boasted that no other building in this period of history had anything like five storeys. Then he was on to the fascinating subject of aqueducts and sewers. June found herself concealing a yawn. To her horror, Cosmo saw her.

'And now I think we've earned a drink,' he said quickly as they joined the other aliens on the balcony above the courtyard, looking down on the duelling humans. June felt nervous about mingling with such extraordinary-looking creatures, but the Doctor seemed to take it in his stride and she didn't want to embarrass him. There were one-eyed aliens and horse-like aliens and aliens with faces like lions and sprouting enormous wings. They wore elegant dinner clothes, sipped elegant drinks and gossiped and giggled elegantly. Some passed comment on the human combatants down in the square, but the fighting seemed more like background entertainment, like a telly on at a party. June felt embarrassed at her own bedraggled state. She wasn't even wearing any shoes.

'This is the main arena,' Cosmo continued, leading them up to the balcony. He nodded and smiled at some of the guests, holding his head high to show he was on official business. 'The late human period preferred an eye-shaped game space, of course. They staged gladiatorial contests, pitched players against wild animals and – most savage of all – fought a game called "football". Its rules are lost to us now, but it sounds absolutely ghastly!'

'Ghastly?' said June. 'Why?'

'Well,' said Cosmo, leaning towards her conspiratorially. 'We don't know exactly. But one source claims they competed for two hours, during which not one player died!' He gurgled with laughter as if this was the funniest thing in the world. 'Seriously, though,' he said. 'Most respected academics don't think that would have been tenable.'

June smiled up at him, horrified but trying not to show it. A spiky waiter in a silk bow tie glided round them with a tray of drinks. Deukalion leaned in and grabbed a glass of a scarlet liquid. He made to drain it but the Doctor stopped him just in time. The glass was returned to the tray.

'Wallagula dissolves human stomachs,' he explained.

'Great!' enthused Deukalion. 'Just what I'm after.'

'Go watch the competitors,' the Doctor told him. 'I'll need tips for laying a wager.' When Deukalion was gone, the Doctor turned to Cosmo. 'Primitives,' he said.

'Oh, I know,' agreed Cosmo easily. 'Who'd think they'll grow up to be the scourge of the galaxy!'

'What?' said June. 'Human beings?'

'No offence,' Cosmo added hastily. 'Some of my best friends are humans.'

'Really?' said the Doctor.

'Oh yeah,' said Cosmo. 'Well, there's you two, anyway.'

'We end up the scourge of the galaxy?' said June, appalled.

'Tell me, Cosmo,' the Doctor interrupted. 'What year are you from? In the future, I mean?'

Cosmo scratched at his forehead with one enormous

claw. 'The Lord Predator, Haralto Wong Bopz Wim-Waldon Arlene, died twenty-two years ago. The current Lord Predator prevails.'

'Yes, he prevails,' agreed the Doctor airily. 'Thank you.' He leaned over to June. 'He's from the year 34,600 or so. Bit after the Platonic War.' He considered a moment. 'And, sorry, personal question. Have the Slitheen been allowed back home yet?'

Cosmo gasped at the Doctor. He looked quickly round at the assembled alien guests, but they were all too busy with one another. Cosmo cleared his throat. 'I can't imagine what nasty rumours you've heard about my family,' he sniffed.

'I'm sure they're all completely unfounded,' said the Doctor.

'But also tricky to disprove,' admitted Cosmo, his head sagging down. 'We expect a legal ruling any time in the next thousand years.'

'Oh, sure,' said the Doctor. 'So at the moment you're temporarily of no fixed abode. Looking for opportunities. On the make, so to speak.'

'The Slitheen have always been entrepreneurs,' Cosmo told him carefully.

'Oh yeah,' grinned the Doctor. 'This is very impressive. I'm just trying to build up a picture. Make a great feature, you see. You and the family, battling all the odds. Coming up with this lot from nothing. Great stuff for an editorial.'

Cosmo snickered. 'That could be a valuable advertisement for what we're doing here.'

'I suppose it might be,' nodded the Doctor. 'Though

obviously you know the rules. It would have to look like I was being independent.'

'Oh yes,' drawled Cosmo. 'I completely understand. Tell me, Doctor, what else would you like to see?'

The Doctor looked all round, popping his mouth like a goldfish. 'I dunno really,' he said. 'The accommodation – for the guests *and* the competitors. The transporter systems you're using. The temporal drives for getting back to Arlene-plus-22. Everything you've got.'

Cosmo blinked at him and for a moment June thought the Doctor had pushed him too far. Then Cosmo grinned wickedly, showing his long, razor-sharp teeth. 'You're planning a very big editorial,' he said.

'Well, I can't promise anything,' warned the Doctor. 'But I could pitch this as a main feature.'

'Then please,' crooned Cosmo, 'come this way.'

The Doctor grinned at June and followed behind the Slitheen as he led them through the throng of aliens.

June turned back to the balcony. 'Deukalion!' she called.

He came running over. 'I don't like how the rest of the competitors look up at me on the balcony,' he said. 'I haven't touched the drinks up here, but I don't think they're going to buy that stuff about us all being in this together.'

'We'll get through to them,' June told him. 'It's going to be OK.'

'So you say,' said Deukalion. 'But—' His eyes opened wide. 'Eep!'

A huge, broad-chested man barred their way. He looked like he worked out – a lot. Long golden hair reached down to his shoulders, his skin glistening like scales. His neck boasted long grey slashes of skin, and he glided towards them not on legs but a glistening, fishy tail. He was some kind of alien merman.

'Um, excuse me,' he said to June. 'Are you an indigenous Terran native?'

June furrowed her brow at him. 'Sorry,' she said kindly, 'I don't know what that means. And we kind of have to be somewhere. Catch you later, maybe.'

She grabbed Deukalion's hand and they pushed past the merman to catch up with the Doctor and Cosmo.

'He fancied you!' Deukalion insisted as they hurried up the gangway.

'He didn't!' June replied, but could feel herself blushing. What would a merman see in a plain human girl like her anyway?

'I might as well have been invisible,' Deukalion went on. 'I could have been singing the tale of my people and he would only have noticed you.'

'Just drop it,' June told him. 'And don't tell *him*.' They had almost caught up with the Doctor.

'Yeah, but he fancied you,' whispered Deukalion.

'All right, maybe he did,' June said through gritted teeth.

The Doctor turned round to see them coming. June gave him a wide smile.

'Everything OK?' he asked.

'Oh yeah,' she said. 'What have we missed?'

'Well,' said the Doctor, 'we've been discussing these

earthquakes. Cosmo admits they're a nuisance.'

'And they're nothing to do with our operation,' Cosmo added quickly. 'The whole region sits over two tectonic plates.'

'Even so,' the Doctor said. 'It's a tad more seismically active than it should be. Normally you can predict earthquakes and stuff. But you say this lot just comes out of nowhere.'

'We are looking into it,' said Cosmo sadly.

'You mean the earthquakes aren't the work of the masters?' asked Deukalion in amazement.

Cosmo glanced at the Doctor and June before replying. He obviously wasn't used to answering to the natives. 'We are looking into it,' he said.

'But we've made sacrifice in your honour to spare us from them,' said Deukalion. 'You've accepted our offerings. You attended our rituals.'

'Yes, well,' admitted Cosmo, glancing again at the Doctor and June. 'We just wanted to be polite. And the rituals are part of the authentic experience, aren't they?'

'What?' said Deukalion, utterly appalled.

'Humans take their beliefs very seriously,' said June, taking Deukalion's hand. She could see it wouldn't do to annoy the huge Slitheen.

'Oh, we know that,' Cosmo told her. 'And it's not like we charge our parties more for attending the festivities. It's all part of the package. It has mutual benefit.' He appealed to Deukalion. 'We come to these gatherings with your feed.'

'That is true,' admitted Deukalion. 'And we get the wine as well.'

'That's very clever of you,' said the Doctor. 'Making them dependent. Makes them easier to round up.'

'What do you think we are?' said Cosmo, eyes wide. 'We didn't do this to them. We arrived here to find mankind in a wretched state. They scavenged in the ruins of once great cities. They chased after wild cattle and fought each other for meat. They were on the edge of extinction.'

The Doctor narrowed his eyes. 'What happened?'

'I've no idea,' said Cosmo. 'Honestly. But we're not the only non-terrestrials to come this way. The Osirans made quite an impact on the continent just south of here.'

'The pyramids were built a thousand years ago,' said the Doctor.

'Aliens built the pyramids?' asked June.

'No,' said the Doctor. 'Humans built the pyramids. But aliens gave them a few pointers.' He gazed up at Cosmo. 'So you're saying that since then humanity has just declined?'

'I don't know,' said Cosmo. His round, black eyes twinkled. 'Maybe there's another feature in it. You can visit some of the farms we've set up ourselves. They're very picturesque.'

'Maybe,' said the Doctor. 'So you found starving masses and you gave them all they needed.'

'We use molecular repurposing,' said Cosmo proudly, indicating the bracelet on his wrist. 'Point this at the raw sand or rock and you can turn it into grain. They don't grow it themselves, of course. Poor things don't know how. So we pop round on a regular basis and make sure they don't run out.'

'But then they won't learn!' said June.

Cosmo blinked in confusion. 'They've no intention of learning.'

'Why bother growing it when it's just dumped on your doorstep?' said the Doctor.

'Exactly,' said Deukalion. 'Anyway. Farming's dirty. You spend all day in the muck.'

June felt her head reeling. She knew farming was crucial to history. She remembered all the dull stuff about the wool trade and enclosures she'd had to learn for her A levels. Even in her own day, the ways people farmed, how they managed to feed themselves, was always in the news. And these aliens were stopping them doing it.

'But they've got to farm for themselves,' she told Cosmo, her voice high with emotion. 'They won't be sustainable otherwise.'

'Ah,' grinned Cosmo. 'That's an important word. Make sure you mention it in your article, Doctor. The tourists we bring here provide the revenue to finance what we do. That's what these wet-hearted naysayers don't understand. They write letters and chain themselves to our time drives, saying we shouldn't interfere in history. But the humans here don't know any better. With the best will in the world, they're not very bright. And if we stop doing this, if we stop bringing tourists, all the humans round the Mediterranean will starve.'

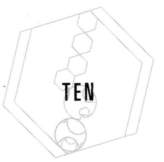

TEN

They continued the tour in silence. Cosmo pointed out the plush quarters that catered to the needs of eighty-seven per cent of all known alien species. The Doctor admired things called puffer amps or something. But June wasn't really listening.

Instead she turned the issues over in her mind. Perhaps Cosmo had a point. Yes, she wanted the aliens gone and for human beings to take charge of themselves. But they couldn't do that in one sweeping movement without thousands of people starving to death. This needed a long-term solution, involving a widespread programme of education and training. And she couldn't get involved in anything like that herself. She had her own life to get back to.

And if *she* wasn't prepared to put the work in, to save the future of her own species, why should anyone else?

'We have to do something,' she told the Doctor.

'What do we do?' he said.

'I don't know, we tell someone,' she said.

'That's what his article's going to do,' Cosmo pointed out. 'Give them all the facts. Let them make up their own minds.'

'Um,' said Deukalion. 'Sorry. What is this article you keep going on about? I hear the word and I imagine a clay tablet with writing. But for more than just keeping records of our food stocks.'

'It's a sort of song,' June told him. 'A story you tell other people. But you write it down.'

Deukalion nodded. 'But why can't you just sing it?'

Cosmo nudged June's elbow. 'I wouldn't bother,' he said. 'Even the simple stuff's beyond them. You just go round in circles.' He gestured up the passageway. 'We're nearly at the transporter booth that blinks us across to admin. You can see our temporal technology there.'

'Brilliant,' said the Doctor. 'I love a bit of that.'

Deukalion shrugged at June as they lagged behind. 'I understand the words,' he said. 'But the meaning just sounds bar-bar bar-bar bar-bar.'

'It's easy, really,' said the Doctor. 'You've got a room with a map on the wall, right?'

'That's right,' Cosmo confirmed.

'Right,' said Deukalion, brow creased as he tried to understand.

'The map,' said the Doctor, 'is covered in little red dots. You choose the red dot you want to go to. You press it. And zzzip! you're there.'

'It's more *ping!* you're there,' said Cosmo. 'But all right, that's how it works.'

'You understand?' June asked Deukalion.

He grinned. 'Not a bit of it.'

'But I understand the language,' said June. She looked at the Doctor. 'Your ship is translating for me, isn't it?'

'Yeah,' said the Doctor. 'But Deukalion lacks the conceptual vocabulary. Imagine going back to the 1860s and finding the world's leading physicist. Then explain to him about compact discs. You shine a light at a small, round mirror and out comes all this old music. These people haven't even invented the wax cylinder. They'd think you were a witch.'

'Aren't you a witch?' said Deukalion.

'No!' said June.

'You talk like one,' he said sheepishly.

'She smells like one,' gurgled a low voice from up ahead. They all turned to stare up the dark passageway.

'Oh,' said Cosmo, sniffing deeply. 'This is a treat. My siblings have popped over from the administrative centre. Hello, Mamps and Hisk and Leeb! These are my new friends.'

'Hello!' said the Doctor cheerily.

Three Slitheen lumbered out of the gloom. If anything, they were even taller and fatter than Cosmo, their claws and teeth more sinister. One of them, with a gold ring through its nose, waggled a claw at Cosmo.

'Cosmata,' it gurgled crossly. 'What are you doing with these prey?'

'They're not, Mamps, they're not,' Cosmo said quickly,

waving his claws in caution. 'You can tell they're from the future. Sniff their clothes and hormones.' He turned back to the Doctor, June and Deukalion. 'My big sister,' he said.

'How do you do,' said the Doctor.

Mamps inhaled carefully. 'Mmm, you've been around a bit, haven't you?' she slurred. 'I can taste the nymph glands of the planetoid Gris in the fibres of your suit.'

'Very good,' said the Doctor. 'I was there a few billennia from now. Anyway. As Cosmo already knows, I'm doing this feature on your operation.' He waved his wallet of magic paper in front of their wide, black eyes. 'It's for the *Mutter's Spiral Herald*…'

'Really,' said Mamps. 'So you'll want access to all our systems.'

'Well,' said the Doctor, 'just a quick nose round. What you're doing here is just fascinating. Isn't it fascinating, June?'

'Fascinating,' she agreed.

'Hmm,' Mamps considered, taking a step forward. Then she lashed out a claw, catching the Doctor round the neck and lifting him from his feet.

'No!' cried June.

'But we've done this already,' said Deukalion. 'I don't understand.'

'He'll only give us a bad write-up!' whined Cosmo.

'He's not a journalist,' sneered Mamps. 'He doesn't smell sour enough. And he's using psychic paper to confuse our minds.'

'It helps,' the Doctor wheezed, his own eyes bulging from their sockets as Mamps squeezed his slender neck.

'Me. Get my. Stories.'

'You *are* a wriggly specimen,' cooed Mamps, lifting him closer to inspect him. 'And I don't smell any fear. Defiance, yes. But you're not scared at all.'

She let go her grip and the Doctor smacked hard into the ground.

June ran to where he lay. Deukalion came to join them, cowering behind June. The Doctor gazed up at the four Slitheen that closed around them, brandishing their claws.

'This isn't how you get your five stars,' he said, hoarsely.

'Oh,' preened Mamps, 'I like him. He fights even at the end.'

'He seemed very convincing,' said Cosmo in a small voice.

'I told you,' said Mamps. 'The agitators have all kinds of tricks to inveigle their way into what we're doing.'

'Agitators?' protested June. 'We're not agitators.'

'Oh, come on,' said Cosmo. 'You were asking all about the welfare of the human prey.'

'You hunt people?' she said, horrified.

'They're Slitheen,' the Doctor told her.

'We have to pay for the humans' food somehow,' said Cosmo. 'We take a small percentage of them each year. And those provide entertainment which draws the tourists and their revenue.'

'You hunt us down,' said Deukalion in horror. This was evidently news to him too. 'We're meant to be competing.'

'And you are,' said Mamps. 'There are games and levels. We give you a sporting chance. The odds are better than for your surviving without our patronage. Really, I could run you the numbers but you wouldn't understand them.'

'It's barbaric,' spat June.

'It's your heritage,' said Mamps.

June felt suddenly cold. 'What does she mean?' she asked the Doctor.

'It's a theme park,' he said. 'You saw those costumes everyone was wearing. The policewomen who didn't have shoes. This place lets aliens see the dark past of humanity. Their battles. The gladiatorial games.'

'That's the word!' laughed Mamps. 'That's the very word. I said it would come to me!' She twisted round to address her siblings. 'That needs to go on the posters. We've resurrected Earth's famous gladiators.'

She gazed down at the humans on the ground beneath her. Thick saliva drooled at them from her lips. 'And I've had another idea,' she said. 'This Doctor is in the next show.'

ELEVEN

The waiting was the worst part. The Doctor, June and Deukalion were locked in a damp cell, the sounds of the courtyard being prepared echoing through the one high, tiny window. The preparations sounded complex and enormous. Whatever the Slitheen had planned, it looked like it would be spectacular.

June huddled up against the wall, trying to think about anything but what she knew of gladiatorial contests staged by the ancient Romans. They had staged enactments of great battles, hunted lions and elephants, generally done anything they could think of that involved exciting deaths. Some of her classmates – mostly the boys – had revelled in the gory details. It didn't feel quite so much fun when you were one of the competitors.

'It's going to be fine,' said the Doctor for the umpteenth time. 'We're going to get out of this.'

'So what's the plan?' said June.

Before the Doctor could answer, Deukalion shook his head. 'We all stick together,' he said sarcastically. 'Yeah, that's going to work. You'd think they'd at least let the condemned have a last amphora of wine.'

He punched the wall, then, pretending it hadn't hurt, placed his sore hand under his armpit.

June sat quietly, thinking of all she'd left behind, back in her own time. Where would her mum even start when June failed to come home? Would there be missing-person posters and an appeal on the telly? What would Bruno and Melissa make of it, her treacherous ex-boyfriend and ex-best mate? She felt a guilty thrill at what it would do to them. And then felt even more guilty for thinking it. None of that seemed to matter any more.

The man in the suit of armour came to release them from the cell. He had with him a squad of guards in various not-quite-right historical costumes, brandishing swords and spears to ensure June and the others didn't try anything.

'Sorry,' he said. 'It's time.'

They were led from their cell and, as they got nearer to the great courtyard, they could hear the assembled crowd. The gurgling voice of one of the Slitheen boomed over the loudspeaker system, whipping the audience of assembled aliens up into a frenzy.

'You've only two minutes left to place your bets,' it said. 'We're now nine to one against on them surviving ninety seconds. But these are wily human beings. Surely some of you fought in the Platonic War or have done the tour of New Mars. You know what these people are like! My colleagues are ready to accept all currencies…'

Up ahead, June saw the bright opening leading out on to the courtyard. They had dusted the courtyard with bright yellow sand. It made it look more like an athletics arena. The ghoulish thought struck her that it would also help soak up any blood. Her heart hammered in her chest and she struggled just to breathe. Deukalion looked no better, but the Doctor didn't seem worried at all. That confidence, that mad bravado, helped settle her nerves. Yes, they were in this together. And, whatever the odds, she trusted him.

'Sword or spear?' asked the man in the suit of armour.

'Oh, I'm fine as I am,' said the Doctor.

'What?' asked Deukalion. 'Are you mad?'

'Maybe,' said the Doctor. 'I just don't like weapons.'

The man in the suit of armour nodded. 'It means it will be quick,' he said. He turned to June. 'Sword or—'

'I'm fine, too,' June cut in.

The Doctor beamed. 'Good for you.'

'We're in this together, aren't we?' she said, taking his arm.

'Well I'm going to have both,' said Deukalion sniffily.

'You're not allowed both,' said the man in the armour.

'But they've not got weapons, so it evens out,' said Deukalion.

'He's right,' said the Doctor. 'Not that it's going to do him any good. But, on average, you give him both and we've still got less than one weapon each.'

The man in the armour considered, then sighed, shaking his head. Deukalion was given a long, bronze sword and a spindly, wobbling spear. He could barely lift either of them, so he dragged them behind him as he followed the Doctor and June out into the light.

They knew the audience had seen them by the sudden explosion of noise. Cheering, applauding, the slap of tentacle and flesh against the floor and balustrade. June blinked in the sunlight, glancing round at the packed balconies. Aliens even sat on the tiled roof to get a better view. She had been to football matches once or twice, had heard the same roar of the crowd. They were baying for her blood.

The Doctor led her and Deukalion out to the centre of the courtyard where a tall Slitheen was standing. June recognised Cosmo's brother Hisk, sporting a top hat and glittering bow tie.

'That's it, that's it,' Hisk slurred appreciatively. 'Come and say a few words for our dear viewers.'

He poked a silver prong of a microphone under the Doctor's nose. The Doctor gazed round at the aliens, milking the moment. Then he leant into the microphone. 'You should all be ashamed of yourselves,' he said.

The aliens laughed delightedly, some of them even applauded.

'Dear me, you're a natural,' said Hisk. 'We like a bit of spirit. But tell me, competitor, what fighting style can we expect to see?'

'We're not going to fight,' said the Doctor simply. Several of the audience laughed at this, but most shuffled uncomfortably in their seats.

'Oh, very good,' crowed Hisk, though he also looked

uncomfortable. He pointed the microphone at the ground as he whispered, 'You know what we'll do to your kingdom if you don't play along?'

'I don't have a kingdom,' said the Doctor. 'And we're not going to play your game.'

The huge Slitheen blinked at him. For a moment June thought Hisk might just strangle the Doctor there and then. But he lifted the microphone and giggled into it. 'Oh, we've got a feisty one here, ladies and gentlemen. He's saying he's not going to fight! He's going to be a pacifist in the ring!'

The audience took the bait and began to laugh.

'I'm giving you one chance,' the Doctor told Hisk. 'Let us go now, stop all this. Or I will have to stop you.'

Hisk looked him up at down. 'You?' it said.

'Me,' said the Doctor. And even June felt scared by the way he said it.

The Slitheen snorted, though he was obviously disturbed. He backed away from the Doctor. 'The competitor says this is my last chance,' he told the crowd. 'But let's see what he makes of tonight's first challenger...' He hurried through a gate which closed behind him, the crowd applauding and cheering.

Across the courtyard, another gate slowly opened. June could hear something roaring and grunting behind it, something huge and angry. Then a huge black bull barrelled out towards them.

The bull was at least as tall as she was, maybe the size of a minivan. Long, sharp horns curled from either side of its enormous head. Beady eyes fixed on June and the others. It scraped its front hoof in the sand, lowering its head, ready to charge. The crowd roared its approval.

'I'm ready,' said Deukalion, coming forward with his spear. 'You two keep back.'

'Deukalion,' said the Doctor. 'We won't win by fighting. We just become part of their game.'

'We've got to do something,' June told him. 'That thing's enormous!'

'And stupid,' said the Doctor.

'And angry,' said Deukalion. 'It's coming!'

The bull had started to trot towards them, slowly picking up speed. The Doctor stood his ground. June and Deukalion sank back behind him, utterly terrified. The bull brayed a low, guttural challenge as it began to run. The Doctor smacked his lips.

'You're not convincing anyone,' he said.

'Doctor!' said June.

'It's fine,' he said. 'I've thought of something. Well, to be honest, you did.' And he started running headlong at the bull.

June gaped in horror. The Doctor raised his hands above his head and started shouting. The crowd watching were on their feet, delighted. June couldn't breathe. The huge blocky shape of the bull charged down on the Doctor and he kept sprinting towards it. The bull lowered its head, its huge horns outstretched…

And the Doctor grabbed them. The bull lifted its head, and the Doctor leapt, somersaulting over the bull's back and landing neatly in the sand.

'Olé!' he shouted.

And the crowd went absolutely mad, on their feet applauding. June and Deukalion were applauding too.

The bull skidded to a stop and looked round, confused. It saw the Doctor, bowing gracefully to his audience, and grunted with annoyance. Head down, horns pointed right at him, it began to run.

The Doctor didn't see it, too busy with taking the applause. June took a step forward, ready to cry out. But then she saw the Doctor hesitate. The bull barrelled towards him and, at the last minute, the Doctor put his arms back, caught the horns again and flipped backwards over its back, managing two complete twists in the air before he landed on his feet.

The audience were ecstatic. Again the bull skidded round and this time the Doctor flipped over its back one-handed. 'Come on!' he shouted at the bull. 'That one was too easy!'

The bull stopped, panting, sweat glistening in its thick black fur. Up in the balconies, aliens gabbled excitedly and exchanged slips of paper. Against all the odds, the Doctor had survived more than ninety seconds. Bulbs flashed as the tourists took pictures.

The bull remained perfectly still, head low, its breathing ragged. Slowly, the Doctor began to walk towards it. He spoke gently to it, too quietly for June to hear the words. But she saw the bull take a step gingerly forward. The Doctor reached a hand out and began to stroke the bull's shaggy forehead. The bull responded, pressing its face against his side.

'Awww,' said a large part of the crowd.

The Doctor looked round to grin at them as he stroked the bull behind the ears.

'Um,' said Deukalion, and he dropped the spear so it slapped into the sand.

'Yeah,' said June. 'He's good.'

A spattering of applause broke out from in amongst the crowd. The sound grew, more and more aliens picking it up. Soon, the Doctor and the tamed beast had earned a standing ovation. And the squawking fury of Hisk.

The Slitheen charged out into the sandy courtyard waving an angry claw. 'This just isn't on,' he yelled at the Doctor. 'It's against all the rules. We're contractually obliged to show a fatality. It's either you or this stupid cow!'

The Doctor turned slowly. 'You're making a mistake,' he called to him.

'Mistake?' Hisk exploded. 'Mistake?' He was almost on them now. 'I've *got* to have a death. It's what the audience expects!'

His voice was shrill, his claws up in the air as he emphasised the point. The bull chose its moment and charged.

'No, wait!' cried the Doctor as the bull pushed past him.

June saw him fall back, rolling nimbly out of the way of the hooves. Hisk cried out, tried to get his claws down and round in time. But too late! The audience gasped as the bull smashed into him.

June turned quickly away.

TWELVE

They were put back into the same cell as before. Deukalion punched the wall again, then slipped his bruised knuckled under his armpit.

'Well, you started well,' said June to the Doctor who sat dolefully in one corner.

'I thought I could show them a better way,' said the Doctor. 'But the Slitheen won't forgive me for killing one of their own.'

'So we're just on to the next level,' said June.

'Perhaps,' said the Doctor. 'Or they'll just take us out of the game. I'm sorry, June. I miscalculated.'

'You were brilliant out there,' she told him.

He smiled. 'Yes, I suppose I was.' But the darkness still haunted his eyes.

Eventually Cosmo came to see them. The young Slitheen hung his head sadly. His face looked bruised dark green.

'The family is very upset with you,' he snivelled. 'We all felt those horns.'

'I'm sorry,' said the Doctor. 'I really am. I tried to warn him.'

'Hmm,' Cosmo said. 'Not very hard. Let's just hope the insurance pays out. He had a partner and eggs.'

'I'm sorry,' said the Doctor again. 'What are you going to do with us?'

Cosmos shifted uncomfortably. 'I know what I'd *like* to do,' he said. 'It's been days since I hunted anything. But Mamps says that we have to acknowledge your appeal.'

'I haven't appealed,' said the Doctor.

'No, your appeal,' said Cosmo. 'Your showbiz style and panache. The customers are always right.'

'You mean your tourists liked the show?' asked June.

'They loved it,' said Cosmo sadly. 'You do everything you can for these people, literally slave day and night. And what really makes them happy? One of your brothers getting skewered!'

'It's not very grateful, is it?' said June.

'No,' said Cosmo. 'It's not. Anyway. They want you at the banquet tonight.'

'A banquet?' asked Deukalion, suddenly perking up. 'In the Doctor's honour?'

'Of course not,' said Cosmo. 'We have a banquet every night. But some of our guests want to see you. Mamps hopes it will shut them up if we stick you on one of the tables.'

'What do you expect me to tell them?' asked the Doctor.

'Will there be wine?' asked Deukalion.

'You'll behave yourself,' Cosmo warned the Doctor. 'That's all. Or I'll skewer both your friends.'

The banquet consisted of four rows of long tables crowded with all kinds of what June assumed to be food. Alien tourists chattered and bickered and shoved past each other to reach the various delicacies, loaded high on their plates. They turned as June, the Doctor and Deukalion were led in by Cosmo. Some applauded, some catcalled, some laughed. Because they'd turned, she could see what they'd been eating. The huge, severed head of a bull stared blindly from the end of the table. June felt her stomach heave.

Cosmo led them to a separate, small table on which were strewn a few meagre scraps of cooked meat. There were similar scraps all over the floor, as June's bare feet soon discovered. The Doctor suggested that they might want a proper meal, and Cosmo muttered that he'd see what was available.

As soon as he was gone, aliens began to crowd their little table. They wanted pictures or autographs or to ask questions. June kept being asked how long she'd been married to the Doctor. Bulbs flashed up close, blinding her, and she found herself signing her name across holograms of her own startled face.

The Doctor chattered happily to the queuing aliens. 'They're fascinated by humanity,' he told June. 'You're all so exotic and strange. I think this lot could help us change things around here.'

June didn't like the attention – she'd never understood

the celebrity thing. At school, she had felt awkward and tongue-tied just having to speak in front of her classmates. But the Doctor's words made her try her best, for the sake of all the humans living under the Slitheen. It wasn't exactly easy.

One alien just wanted to rub its mandibles over the back of her hand. She withdrew quickly, with a squeak of horror. The Doctor leant into her ear.

'He's just showing subservience,' he explained. 'The Aru are a bit touchy-feely.'

June sighed and extended her arm. The Aru leaned forward and shook its chins at her. When it had finished, her wrist felt warm and waxy, but didn't seem to be harmed. 'Thank you,' she told the Aru, who skipped happily away, back to its friends.

She listened in to the Doctor, holding court. The aliens had plenty of questions – how humanity had come from their current primitive state to conquer so much of space, whether they were right to clear the worlds of Pif, or what their role had been in the outbreak of the Platonic War. Smiling the whole time, the Doctor feinted and parried, dodging what were evidently controversial topics. June realised with a start that humanity had a lot to answer for in the future. These people were thrilled and tantalised by contact with humans, but also a little terrified.

Once they'd eaten, Mamps took to the stage to explain the itinerary for the next day. The Slitheen would be attending to some personal business first thing – the funeral of poor Hisk – but they'd be back mid-morning to lead an excursion to the ruined Osiran spaceport. 'Doctor

Romain has prepared handouts and a lecture,' said Mamps, indicating a tall, lithe creature with dreadlocks at the head of one of the tables. 'She's promised to keep it short.'

Then the banquet was over. The tables were cleared around them and a disco was set up. June tried to stay close to the Doctor, but aliens clustered around him, still effervescent with questions. Instead she tried to find Deukalion again, assuming he'd be at the bar.

'Excuse me,' said a voice behind her. She turned to see the huge merman who'd approached her earlier that day. 'I'm sorry,' he said. 'I didn't mean to alarm you.'

June realised her mouth was hanging open. The merman wore a shawl of thin black material that only emphasised his muscles. He slithered towards her on his fishy tail.

'I'm Cecrops,' he said. 'From the Collective of Mulch.'

'I'm June,' she said. 'From Birmingham, at the moment.'

'I tried to speak to you earlier,' said Cecrops. 'I was hoping for your perspective.'

'Oh,' said June. 'OK. What did you want to know?'

'I'm not sure I want to know anything,' said Cecrops as if it were a clever joke. 'I just want to hear it from you. As a native, so to speak. Your testimony should be a part of the discourse.'

She stared at him. 'I don't understand,' she said.

'Right,' he said, smiling sheepishly. 'Well, I guess it's the whole debate about the impact we're having by coming here. I thought you'd have your own view.'

'Do you mean like eco-tourism?' asked June. Either the TARDIS couldn't quite translate his words properly or he was just talking nonsense.

'Yeah, that sort of thing,' he said. 'And also, I just really like human beings. You know?'

She didn't know quite how to answer that. He seemed desperately keen for her to like him. And he was really very good-looking, even with the fishy tail. But he was one of those boys who saw her as the embodiment of some ideal rather than a person in herself. She was a cause for him to champion, not a girl who he might buy a drink.

'Look,' she said. 'I'm sort of with this bloke.' She looked round for the Doctor. He still stood surrounded by aliens, but Mamps had her long arm tightly around him, her golden nose stud sparkling. June made to hurry over to them but Cecrops grabbed her arm.

'I don't take part in the hunts,' he told her. 'And I'm a vegan.'

June gasped in horror at him. She must have looked so appalled that he let her go. She twisted away from him, running for the Doctor, stood there with the Slitheen. Their enormous claws loomed at her as she approached. She wanted to be sick. It hadn't occurred to her that humans might be on the menu. If the Doctor had lost to the bull that afternoon, would this banquet have included him? The odd looks the aliens had given her all through dinner suddenly made sense. She reached the Doctor, head spinning.

'They kill us!' she said. 'They're killing us.'

Mamps leaned into her. 'Not right at this moment, I think you'll agree.' The alien tourists squawked with amusement.

June found the Doctor had taken her hands in his. She looked up into his dark eyes and immediately she felt better. He smiled, a look that said 'I know' and 'I'm going to put this right.'

He turned to face Mamps. 'But you are killing us,' he said. 'That's what the games are about.'

Mamps wavered for a moment. She glanced at the alien tourists. 'Oh,' she said. 'You say that now. But just like everyone else, you volunteered to compete.' She bent her head down to conspire with one of the tourists. 'Honestly. They say it's for the honour of their tribes. It's really quite delicious!'

June wanted to punch her, to do something stupid and futile, but the Doctor held on to her hand.

'I suppose,' he said, 'you tell them we don't feel pain like you do.'

Mamps swung round to face him. 'How did you—' she began. And then she remembered the eyes watching her and broke into a smile.

'He's got ideas about what we can do to improve the lot of the humans in our care,' she gurgled. 'And we at Slitheen Excursions are very keen to hear his point of view. I know many of you have concerns about the environmental footprint our tours leave behind them. Honestly, we share those concerns. And that's why the Doctor's going to be our ambassador. We'll show him everything he asks to see. And he can then advise us on where we can improve.'

The aliens applauded. Deukalion reached out to hand June a wide-necked goblet of wine, a *kylix* like she'd seen in museums. Cecrops slithered up beside her and joined in the applause. June felt trapped, confused. Had the Doctor just talked his way into the Slitheen's operation? Were they really asking him to advise them?

She saw Mamps lean back to whisper to Leeb, the last of Cosmo's siblings. Leeb snickered and hurried away. Mamps turned back to gaze at the Doctor with dark and greedy eyes.

The Doctor came over to June and Deukalion. 'Well,' he said loudly, 'it's all going a lot better than we could have expected. I'm going to pop over to the island where they've got whatever they're using to bring people here from the future. You're going to be their guests here while I'm gone.'

'But—' began June. The Doctor put his arm around her companionably.

'I know you're going to miss me,' he said and hugged her.

'It's a trap,' she whispered in his ear.

He held her close. 'I know,' he said. 'They need me away from the alien fan club before they can have their revenge. But what else can we do?'

'Doctor!' she said, holding on to him tightly.

He withdrew from her, smiling brightly, that cunning look in his eye.

THIRTEEN

The Doctor stepped out of the transmat and looked all around him. 'That was very smooth,' he told Mamps and Cosmo, who had materialised beside him. The Doctor ran his tongue round his teeth. Journeys by localised transmat always left a taste in his mouth like liquorice. It tasted like he'd been moved about seventy miles due north. A small part of his brain thought this might be important, that it should connect to some other loose bit of memory he'd picked up some time in the last 900 years. He decided it would come back to him if it was important. There were more pressing concerns.

They had arrived in a wide room cut smoothly through bare rock. He'd seen something like it in a palace of giant termites. Or it reminded him of the Jubilee line on 24 June 2006, when he'd had that ice cream. In fact, the Jubilee line could be a lot like a palace of termites, depending on what time you were there. His mind whirring, the Doctor began to nose round, inspecting the controls and readouts in the wall. And ignoring the two huge Slitheen. They might be planning to sneakily kill him but he wasn't going to make it easy.

'Atmospheric controls look fine,' he told them. 'Air's a little muggy, but we should be OK. It'll get the creases out of my suit. Um… Is this a hard-hat area? Been ages since I wore a hard hat.'

'Indeed,' said Mamps, not listening. 'The temporal drives are up this way.'

He followed them up the passageway. They didn't seem that worried about keeping an eye on him, which he felt was a little rude. He knew they wanted to kill him out here. They knew that he knew. He knew that they knew that he knew… It was all about the optimum moment to actually do the deed. With a start, he realised that they thought it was a game. They were like cats teasing a mouse. Well, he'd have to see about that.

They continued up the passageway. The Doctor's trainers squeaked on the smooth floor. He found he could make them squeak even more if he dragged his feet. The noise annoyed Mamps, who gritted her teeth. But the Doctor glanced at Cosmo, who looked like he wanted to laugh. Divide and conquer: simple.

The passageway opened out onto a wide viewing gantry, overlooking vast machines. His eyes danced over them, quickly identifying the different systems and the ways they'd been modified. The gantry led off to a series of control panels and the open space where tourists from the future would materialise. He liked that you got to see the workings of the temporal drive as the first step on the tour.

Eager to distract the Slitheen, the Doctor cooed at the awesome sight of the huge machines, though he'd already appraised them in a glance. He went right up to the railing, holding the bar tightly as the two Slitheen came to join him, in case they tried to throw him over the edge right away. How easy, to go back to their tourists and badly act their sorrow at some terrible accident. Perhaps that was why they were playing this out; they didn't want to go back too soon.

'It's a very clever system,' he enthused. 'Cor. Is that a stardrive disseminator bolted to the side?'

Mamps chuckled wetly. 'The very idea,' she said. 'Do you think we built this thing out of string?'

The Doctor nodded, admiring the workings, following the route from the generation and treatment of chronon particles to the thing like a Wurlitzer at the core. 'Did you build it?' he asked, all innocence.

Mamps gripped the railing, her claws clanging against the metal, the sound echoing round the chamber. 'Why do you ask?'

'Oh, don't get me wrong,' said the Doctor. 'Cobbling this together is an achievement in itself. But it's all bits and bobs you've acquired from other people.' He pointed. 'A Navarino time-jump, a Sundayan stabiliser. One of those things that makes the Vortex go wobbly. What are they called again?'

'Doctor,' said Mamps levelly.

'No, I don't think that's it,' said the Doctor. Cosmo giggled at the joke.

'We didn't really bring you here to show you the temporal drives,' said Mamps.

'No, I worked that out, thank you. I'm not half as daft as I look.'

'But you came with us anyway.'

'Yeah,' said the Doctor. 'Probably too trusting. But it's been fascinating to have a look. And I did ask.'

'Consider it a last request,' said Mamps. She grinned cruelly, showing her razor-sharp teeth.

'Well, all right, kill me if you have to,' said the Doctor, and he nonchalantly turned away from her to look back out over the balcony to the huge machines. Mamps reached out her claws to him. But just before she sliced them through his body he shrugged. 'Seems a shame, though,' he said. 'If I'm dead I can't help you out.'

Mamps whipped the claws away behind her back just before he turned back to look at her. She glanced at Cosmo, who grinned at her.

'And what,' she asked the Doctor, 'can you do for the Slitheen?'

'Oh,' said the Doctor. 'I've got a few skills. Make a great curry. Got these long skinny arms if you lose anything down the back of a radiator. Oh, and I can stop your earthquakes.'

Mamps blinked at him. 'My earthquakes?' she said.

'Yeah,' said the Doctor. 'Except they're not really earthquakes. They're the time differential shorting out. Think of them as burps in the system.'

Mamps and Cosmo glanced at one another. 'You can provide evidence for this?'

'Er, yeah,' said the Doctor. 'I think so. If you've got a list of when and where all the earthquakes have taken place?'

'We can get one,' said Mamps.

'Well, it should match up pretty exactly with when you've used the temporal drive. Each earthquake will probably be about nine or ten hours before each use. Nine point five three seven, approximately.'

'Look into it,' Mamps told Cosmo. He bowed and hurried away, his huge fleshy feet slapping on the smooth floor.

The Doctor grinned at Mamps. 'You've been the victim of your own success, haven't you?' he said. 'So many tourists wanting to nose round this period. Cradle of civilisation, or however you've been selling it. But you didn't have so many punters in mind when you had this thing put together.'

Mamps sighed. 'The Navarinos we, um, persuaded to construct it said no more than four transfers per day. We're doing twelve at the moment and can't keep up with demand. There's a waiting list of months.'

'And the Navarinos haven't been able to get the systems to compensate?' said the Doctor, though he already suspected the answer.

Mamps grinned sheepishly. 'After they'd made it work the first time, we sort of ate them.'

The Doctor shook his head. 'That wasn't very clever, was it?' he said.

'It seemed quite clever at the time,' said Mamps. 'Meant

we didn't have to pay them.'

'But it wasn't very forward thinking,' said the Doctor. 'This almighty lash-up just isn't sustainable. And if the thing breaks down, you lot are all trapped here. I don't think that would be good for anyone.'

'We've got a contingency,' said Mamps. 'My siblings in the future can come back to collect us. They've got a time bus for emergencies.'

The Doctor whistled. 'Expensive,' he said.

'Yeah, so it's only to be used in emergencies.' She sniffed and then turned back to look down the corridor. A moment later, Cosmo's footsteps echoed towards them. He emerged from the darkness, belly wobbling as he ran. In his claws he flourished a digital reader.

'He's right!' proclaimed Cosmo as he handed the reader to Mamps. She scrolled the screen, reading the comparison of data. The Doctor noted the readings, surprised at how fast the burps had been growing.

'Yes,' mused Mamps. 'Yes. This is pretty convincing. All the earthquakes accounted for but one.'

'What?' said the Doctor, leaning forward to read the screen. 'Which one?'

'A minor disturbance at sea early this morning. Sank almost a whole shipment of prey.'

'Oh,' said the Doctor, but thought better of revealing that he'd been in that shipment. If they wanted to know where he'd sprung from, they could work it out themselves. 'Well, can't be helped,' he said. 'The odd anomaly here or there. It's the exception that proves the rule!'

'Hmm,' said Mamps. 'We had an exercise on this sort of

thing in causality training.' She tapped her claw against the digital reader, making some quick calculations. 'Yes,' she said. 'The numbers add up. Cosmo run the drive for five-tenths of a second.'

'Wait!' said the Doctor as Cosmo hurried away to the controls. 'You don't need to do that.' He knew he couldn't change anything, that it had already happened. But at the same time he couldn't stand by while they killed all those poor people on the boats. He ran forward to stop Cosmo, but Mamps swept an arm out and threw him skidding across the smooth floor.

'But we do have to do it,' she said. 'The storm happened within the same parameters, so Cosmo must have turned on the drive. It's how time works.' She turned back to Cosmo, stood by the machines. 'Do it!'

Cosmo turned a lever.

'Please!' said the Doctor from where he lay a little stunned on the floor. 'Let me just try to work it out.'

'Too late,' said Cosmo. 'It's done.'

'You killed all those people,' said the Doctor, quietly.

'They were already dead this morning,' said Mamps. 'It's causality. It takes a while to get used to but that's just how things are.' She brought her claws down on him and for a moment he thought she meant to kill him. But the claws stopped above his head and he realised she meant to help him to his feet. He accepted the offer.

'That's all the paradoxes taken care of,' she said. 'Now you can fix it so no one else has to die.'

FOURTEEN

June wandered among the alien tourists, trying to avoid Leeb and Cecrops. Leeb watched her coldly, guarding her while his siblings were away. She could see that he had wicked designs on her, that he considered her his prey. But, weirdly, she felt more bothered by Cecrops, who wouldn't leave her alone. He kept wanting to ask her opinions on various theories and legal arguments relating to interference in human history. She understood his enthusiasm, she ought to have admired it. But she didn't want to be the mascot for his cause. And she found his zeal exhausting. Couldn't he show any interest in her for herself, not as the emblem of a species?

Having finished dinner, she and the alien tourists were back out on the balconies overlooking the main courtyard. Clay braziers burned at regular intervals to keep them warm as they gossiped and drank cocktails. June had asked for a glass of water, but none had been forthcoming. She kept near the braziers, toasting her bare feet.

Humans in historical costume performed down below for their entertainment. They sang, they danced, they wrestled, and the aliens paid them little heed. It seemed they only cared to watch the festivities when there were lives at stake.

June felt numb to it all, drifting through the crowd of aliens to the part of the citadel overlooking the sea. There were no braziers out this far, but she welcomed the cold cutting at her body. Beyond the citadel's walls she could see small communities of houses scattered across the rocky landscape. The sea glinted away in the distance. It should have been a beautiful evening but June felt simply wretched.

She hated being up on this higher tier, looking down on the other humans. And she hated being so helpless. She wanted to shout out, to rail against the aliens and what they'd done to her people. But she also knew that that would do no good. She might as well rage at the sky for all the difference it would make. Causing a fuss might give Leeb the excuse he'd been waiting for.

There had to be another way. But what could she do? She wasn't like the Doctor. She couldn't somersault over wild animals or anything like that. June was just an ordinary, boring girl with no special powers at all.

Deukalion came to join her, but she declined his offer of a *kylix* of wine. She wanted her senses to be sharp. They stood, watching the stars sparkling above them, ignoring the crass laughter of the aliens and the crash of the sea on the cliff beneath the citadel, the sound carried up to them by the still night air.

'The Doctor will be back soon enough,' said Deukalion, though he didn't sound like he believed it.

'He's a match for the Slitheen,' said June. 'He can change all this. Make it right.'

'I hope so.'

'But what do we do if he doesn't come back? It's so vast.'

'We don't stand a chance,' said Deukalion, draining his own *kylix* and starting on the one he'd brought for her. June rolled her eyes and turned away from him, to find Leeb lumbering towards them.

'Hello, dear humans,' he leered, waving his claws in what he probably thought was a friendly gesture. Deukalion let out a squeak of terror and cowered behind June.

'Hi,' said June. 'No word from the Doctor, yet?'

'I'm afraid not,' said Leeb, shaking his head. 'I hope you're not getting bored waiting.'

'We're fine,' said June.

'Good, good,' said Leeb. 'But I thought I'd make a suggestion. Perhaps you'd both volunteer to take part in our next entertainment.'

'What?' said Deukalion. 'I thought I was a local guide! The Doctor needs me.'

'But the Doctor's not here,' said Leeb in a cruel, sing-song voice.

Deukalion whimpered.

June appraised the Slitheen. She and Deukalion were dead anyway, but surely Leeb wouldn't try anything in view of all the tourists. For the moment, he couldn't touch her.

'What's it going to be?' she asked, forcing her own horror down. 'Another wild animal? That didn't work out so well last time.'

Leeb seethed with anger. 'We thought something a little more educational, this time. A re-enactment of the last battle of the Platonic War. You'll like it; the humans win.'

'That doesn't sound so bad,' Deukalion admitted.

'What's the catch?' asked June.

'Catch?' said Leeb. 'Catch? Perish the thought. You two and fifty other competitors putting on a show.'

'Where we have to kill each other,' she said.

'What?' said Deukalion.

'We want it to look authentic,' Leeb gurgled. 'Of course, you could always refuse…'

'Then we refuse,' said Deukalion. 'Oh, now you're going to kill us, aren't you?'

'You can't do anything to us in front of your tourists,' said June. 'They won't like it.'

Leeb considered. 'No,' he said. 'That's true. But no one will see when I do something to your friends.'

'I don't have any friends,' said Deukalion. 'There's a few estranged wives, but do what you like with those.'

Leeb ignored him to blink slowly at June. 'Actaeus,' he said. 'And his daughters. Oh, don't look surprised. We ran a sweep for technology the moment you turned up. We've found your funny blue box.'

'Please,' said June. 'What are you going to do to them?'

'Nothing,' said Leeb. 'If you do as I tell you. Volunteer for the show. Fight and die like you mean it. Make sure there are no awkward questions.'

'There's no way!' laughed Deukalion. 'Is there, June?' He swallowed hard. 'June?'

'What would you do to them?' she asked Leeb.

'Well,' said the tall Slitheen. 'Your friends are up on that rock, aren't they? What will one day be the Acropolis. And underneath is one of our transmat machines. Imagine if there were a problem. Imagine if I accidentally switched off its shield! There'd be the most awful explosion. And for the next thousand years that whole valley would be a nuclear wasteland.'

June gaped at him. 'But you can't!' she said. 'You'd change history. You'd stop humanity ever developing!'

Leeb sighed. 'You think humanity owes everything to the Athenians?'

'Who?' said Deukalion.

June blinked at the huge, green creature. 'Well, no,' she said. 'All kinds of other people played their part. But take the ancient Greeks out of the picture and who knows what the effect could be.'

Leeb scratched at his forehead with the tip of his claw. 'Oh,' he said. 'We were told humans would never get into space if we did anything to this period.'

And June stared in horror at the awful creature. 'Oh no,' she said. 'You know the effect you're having. You're doing it on purpose!'

Leeb smiled. 'Keep your voice down, girl,' it said. 'You're going to behave. You're going to take part in this show. You're going to fight and die with gusto. Our way, humans just grow up without all the war and conquest. You say no and we make them extinct.'

He grinned, showing razor-sharp teeth. 'Your choice.'

'I don't really like heights,' said Cosmo as he clung to the ladder beside the Doctor. They were up at the very top of the cavern, checking the connections of the uppermost machines. Far below them, Mamps watched from the gantry. She seemed quite convinced that there was nowhere else the Doctor could escape to. But he kept glancing round, just in case.

'Me neither,' said the Doctor. He leant backwards from the ladder and began to unscrew the clamps securing one of the devices. 'Best not to think about it,' he said. 'Might help to close your eyes.'

Cosmo closed his eyes, then let out a squeal of horror. 'No,' he said. 'That makes it worse.'

'Oh well,' said the Doctor. 'I'll try not to be too long.'

The huge machines crowded around him and Cosmo. Some of the couplings were really expertly done. He admired the use of a proton valve to join a reintegrator to the shut-out port on an electric black hole. Mamps, he noted, had been talking rubbish. There *was* a stardrive disseminator coiled in a wide loop round the logic gate – a squat, oblong component that looked like a fridge but had an effect on time like a cat-flap. Which meant the Slitheen didn't understand half as much of this system as they liked to make out.

The problem, he'd surmised, was temporal energy leaking out of the system whenever it penetrated space-time. But there were lots of places the leak could be coming from. He'd just have to check every stage…

In doing so, he could check for possible escape routes. Though it didn't make sense for the cave they were in to have any other exits than the one they'd come in by. Made the whole thing secure if they couldn't get out by anything other than the transmats. He could, of course, offer to test the system and transport himself into the future. But then he'd only have all Mamps's siblings asking awkward questions. And June would be left to face the anger of the three Slitheen back here. That didn't really seem fair.

He considered reasons he might need June here alongside him, some expertise she might possess. But even if he could save her, there were still all the humans living round the Mediterranean. There were just too many people involved for him to try any of his usual tomfoolery. His brilliant mind picked over all kinds of possibilities and found flaws in every one.

He'd think of something; he always did. But fixing the machine would at least stop the earthquakes, saving thousands of lives in the process. Best just to get on with the job in hand, then…

But no, that only helped the Slitheen. They would continue bringing tourists back through time and eroding what little chance of taking charge of their own lives the humans had. He couldn't sabotage or blow up the temporal drive because that would strand all the aliens back in time, where they'd get up to all manner of antics. Yes, he could probably take them back to their own time in the TARDIS. But he didn't exactly want to let the Slitheen inside his own ship. He'd had problems with that sort of thing before.

What he really wanted was a way of stopping the temporal drive from working once and for all, but then having it work for him to send everyone home. Which was exactly the sort of paradox he'd always loved untangling. And a wicked thought struck him.

'Oh yes,' he said out loud. 'That would work.'

He released his grip on the ladder and skidded down it at high speed. 'Wheeee!' he called, before hugging his arms around the edges of the ladder to bring him to a stop just before he crashed into the gantry.

'Well?' asked Mamps.

'Oh,' he told her, '*very* well.' He ran to the controls and began punching instructions into them.

By the time Cosmo had climbed down rung by rung to join them, the Doctor had almost finished. Mamps leaned over his shoulder to watch, nodding appreciatively. But if she'd had any idea what he was conjuring, she would have killed him there and then.

'You see?' he asked her as he stepped back from his work.

'Oh yes,' she enthused, patently lying. 'And it will really work?'

'Yeah,' he said, 'I think so. You saw what I did, of course?'

'Should have thought of it myself,' preened Mamps.

Brilliant, he thought, he had them! He turned back to face them. Mamps and Cosmo blocked his way, their green faces leering down at him, showing their razor-sharp teeth.

'It seems,' said Mamps in a girlish, sing-song voice, 'that you're usefulness is at an end.'

'Oh yeah,' said the Doctor. He'd been so busy outfoxing them he'd forgotten they were going to kill him. 'Should have thought of that.'

He grinned. The Slitheen grinned back. And with a terrible roar they pounced.

FIFTEEN

Fifty human beings knelt in the shadows waiting for their cue. Out in the arena, they could just hear Leeb introducing the show, explaining how all the players were willing volunteers. He liked the sound of his own voice too much, but the alien audience seemed to love him.

June knelt in the darkness waiting. She had been cast as one of the aliens, with a crude papier mâché hat with a spindly head attached. While the people playing humans got swords and spears and shields, the 'aliens' were only given wooden props in the shape of ray guns. It didn't look like the war would take very long.

Deukalion cowered beside her, under his own costume hat. Its antennae quivered in time with his quiet sobbing. June reached her hand out to him. He looked up at her, a single tear hanging from his chin.

'I wish the Doctor was here,' he said.

'Yeah,' said June. 'Me, too. He'd know what to do.'

Deukalion shrugged. 'And he said we were in this together.'

June smiled. 'He said we shouldn't fight. But what choice have we got?'

'I used to say that,' said Deukalion. 'I'm governed by impulse, can't help myself. So I drink, I talk to women.' He sighed. 'My first wife says there's always a choice.'

'Not this time,' said June. 'If we don't do this, the whole of history goes *pfft*. The aliens have got a real gripe with humans.'

'Didn't you hear?' said Deukalion. 'The masters said we won. That really annoys some people.'

'The people who lost,' nodded June. 'So they wipe us out back in history, and then we never fight the battle.'

'I wish I was a human,' he said morosely. 'I hate this silly hat.'

And she laughed. 'I think I just had an idea.' She crawled forwards in the darkness, towards the row of people opposite, the competitors who didn't have to wear the papier mâché hats. 'Um, hi,' she addressed them. 'Sorry, my name's June. You're going to think this is weird, but I've had an idea how we can all get out of this alive. And we're all humans, aren't we? We should be in this together.'

The row of figures glanced at one another. A couple of people whispered. And then one of the humans came forward. It took June a moment to recognise her.

'That's what we've been telling them,' said Herse. 'All right, what's the plan?'

***

The aliens – the real aliens – cheered and applauded as the fifty competitors ran out onto the sand of the arena. Those with papier mâché hats made for the right side of the courtyard, those without went left. Leeb introduced them from his place high up on the balcony. After the death of Hisk earlier that day, he'd thought better of standing in the arena himself.

He spoke into the bracelet round his wrist, which amplified his voice, pointing out some of the papier mâché hats. The alien tourists cheered as he named particular species. They also groaned at his cheesy jokes. But Leeb proved a great showman and had the tourists buzzing with excitement for what they were about to see. Their glee bled down into the arena. June trembled with anticipation.

'And so the peace conference of Anselm failed,' cried Leeb, 'the delegates withdrew back to their space fleets. And the war began!'

That was their cue. Twenty-five 'aliens' charged at twenty-five human humans, bellowing and waving their wooden ray guns. The twenty-five humans stood their ground with perfect military discipline. They raised their swords, ready to strike, as the 'aliens' barrelled towards them. June hurled herself across the sand towards Deukalion, right ahead of her. His sword glinted in the moonlight. He looked a lot happier for swapping sides, not having to wear the antennae. And, as she snarled and shouted at him, he gave her a quick wink.

She was almost on him when up went the cry. Herse yelled distinctly a single word. 'Retreat!'

The human humans dropped their swords and fled

around the arena. The 'aliens' pursued them, still shouting and waving their ray guns. Above them, the real aliens gasped in amazement. And then started to applaud.

Deukalion spun round to beg for mercy from June. She grinned, prodding her ray gun forward as if she'd fired it at him. He cried out, clutching his sides, and fell back into the sand. June helped pick off the rest of the fleeing humans.

By the time Herse surrendered, the real aliens were on their feet, whooping and applauding. The dead humans got back to their feet to join the victorious 'aliens' in a bow.

'I think that worked,' grinned Herse to June as the adulation slowly died away.

'We'll see,' said June. Leeb was lumbering down towards them.

'Very good,' he gurgled, clattering his talons together in a strange parody of applause. 'Very ingenious. You changed history for your own amusement.'

'Well, you gave me the idea,' said June.

That really annoyed him. But he glanced back round at the alien tourists, all watching keenly. He couldn't touch her now.

'Your friends on the Acropolis…' he seethed.

'Can wait,' said June. 'You've got something more important to do first.' She nodded at Herse.

'Ladies and gentlemen,' Herse called out, addressing the alien tourists. 'As a token of our esteem, the defeated forces of humanity would like to invite you to join us in the arena for cocktails and canapés.'

Again the alien tourists cheered. Then they began to squabble about how they could get down to the arena.

Leeb gaped. 'But you don't have cocktails or canapés,' he said.

June beamed at him. 'So you'd best rustle something up before they get here,' she said.

Leeb grimaced at her, then pointed the bracelet on his wrist at the sand underneath them. With a high-pitched squeal, the sand began to swirl up in a pink cloud. When the cloud faded away, there was a table laden with drinks and little things to eat. It materialised just in time; the alien tourists descended on the table greedily.

'There,' said Leeb.

'Good,' said June as the alien tourists crowded around them. 'And now,' she said, loudly enough for them to hear, 'we can have a chat about the conditions in which you're keeping us humans.'

As Leeb began to protest, behind his back Deukalion waved from up on the balcony, then disappeared in amongst the aliens.

The Doctor gazed up at the yellowy claws as they slashed towards him. His last thought was of June. And of an overdue library book. And whether he'd be killed instantly or would have a chance to regenerate. And the bleeping of the comms panel, just beside his head.

Mamps lowered her claws with a sigh. 'Oh, really,' she said. 'Get that, will you, Cosmo?'

'Always on call,' said the Doctor.

Mamps shook her head in exasperation. 'I can't be away for a moment.'

Cosmo pressed the button and the screen showed Leeb,

his face pressed up close. 'Mamps!' he said. 'They're being horrid! I don't know what to do.'

Mamps tutted. 'What are you blathering about?'

'The humans,' Leeb told her. 'They've organised a party.'

'You mean like a union?' said Mamps.

'No, a party. With cocktails and stuff.'

'Aw,' said the Doctor. 'I like a good party. Can we go have a look when we're done here?'

Mamps blinked at him. 'You'll be dead when we're done here.'

'Oh yes. Sorry.'

'You can handle a little party,' Mamps told Leeb. 'Let them have their fun.'

'But Mamps,' said Leeb. 'They're talking to the punters. They're talking human rights!'

'What?!?' shrieked Mamps. 'How could you be so stupid? Right, I'll be there in a moment.' She reached out and switched off the communicator. Her nostrils twitched with rage, her golden nose ring glinting.

'Trouble?' said the Doctor cheerily.

'It's none of your concern,' Mamps told him.

'No,' said the Doctor. 'Of course not. You'd better get on with killing me.'

Mamps nodded. 'Yes,' she said, raising one claw above his head.

'Shame though,' said the Doctor just as she was about to strike. 'I've got experience of human rights.'

'I don't give a stuff about human rights,' Mamps told him crossly.

'She doesn't,' Cosmo agreed.

'Yeah,' said the Doctor. 'You're just going to kill them all, aren't you?'

'Yes,' said Mamps. 'I am.'

'Only not in front of your punters,' said the Doctor. 'Because they won't approve of that. So you probably want someone to negotiate for you now.'

Mamps lowered her claws. 'Someone like you, I take it?' she said.

'Well, now you say it,' said the Doctor. 'I suppose I could.'

'Hmm,' said Mamps. 'I let you live and you help us out with this bother. Make the punters think we care for the prey. At least until we can get the prey off somewhere we can kill them without being seen.'

'That sounds like a perfect plan,' said the Doctor. 'And you promise not to kill me if I help you.'

Mamps nodded. 'On my honour,' she said.

'You, er, don't have any honour,' said the Doctor.

Mamps grinned. 'Good point. But we don't have time to draw up a contract. Can't you take my word just this once?'

The Doctor grinned back. 'Tell you what,' he said. 'Why don't I negotiate peace between the humans and tourists, and then we'll see where we are?'

Mamps nodded. 'Yes,' she gurgled. 'That will do fine.'

SIXTEEN

The transmat pinged and four people suddenly stood in the room. Deukalion turned to the others, grinning. They stared at him in awe. He rather liked having pretty women staring at him in awe.

'See?' he said. 'It's easy.'

King Actaeus and his daughters stepped forward, waving their swords at the room as if duelling ghosts. Deukalion sighed and stepped out in front of them. 'There's no one here,' he told them. 'I said it was OK.'

The others did not smile back. 'You foretold the doom of my kingdom,' said Actaeus. The scar running down his face caught the light. 'Told my people to flee for their lives. But we are "OK".'

'No,' said Deukalion. Why did he always have this problem with people in authority? 'I said things would be OK. You didn't need to come back with me.'

'You said you were fighting for the freedom of men,' said Actaeus. 'That the Doctor had sent you. How could we not be here?'

'Well, yeah,' said Deukalion awkwardly. 'Well, we're not fighting exactly. We're being smarter than that.'

The king's daughter-in-law, Aglauros, regarded him with a sly smile. 'The Doctor could talk his way round anyone,' she said.

'Exactly,' said Deukalion. 'So there's no need for you to—'

The map on the wall flickered. Deukalion had survived this far by trusting his instincts. And his instincts were screaming now.

'Quick,' he said, leading the king and his daughters away up the passageway to a storage area. There were crates stacked high on both sides of the corridor, amphorae of wine, olive oil and the liquid fuel he'd seen the masters use for fire. They ducked behind crates filled with fine grey-black dust. Deukalion ducked down behind the crates and his head exploded in a sneeze. He glanced at the king, who could not tear his eyes from the contents of the crates.

'Pepper,' murmured Actaeus. 'More pepper than I've ever seen in my life. We're looking at a fortune!'

Deukalion grabbed him by the shoulder and pulled him down behind the crate. In an instant the magic booth down the passageway let out a ping.

'And,' gurgled a high voice, 'you know what we'll do to you if it doesn't work.'

The Slitheen, Mamps, emerged, another Slitheen tagging along behind her. And behind them both, walking freely, came the Doctor.

'Mamps,' he said cheerfully, 'I fixed your machine, so you can bring all the tourists you want here. And now I'll fix this problem with the humans.'

'I just want you to be conscious of what's hanging on this,' said Mamps. And then she stopped abruptly. She raised her head, sniffing the air. Deukalion peered through the gap between two crates. And Mamps stared directly back at him. Deukalion knew songs in which the masters could sniff out a man like a dog sniffed out prey. His nose twitched again, and he fought back the urge to sneeze. But Mamps gazed at him with her black eyes.

'Something up?' the Doctor asked her.

Her eyes narrowed. Then she looked back at him. 'I think the seasoning is a bit damp,' she said. 'Come on, let's get this done.'

The two Slitheen and the Doctor disappeared down the passageway. A long time after they'd gone, Deukalion dared to let out his breath. He'd never felt so relieved.

'Said we were OK,' he told Actaeus as they got to their feet.

'He's working for them,' Aglauros told him.

'What?' said Deukalion. 'Never. He's spinning them a line.'

'And where did they come from?' said Pandrosos, heading down to the map on the wall.

'It shows the last trip in yellow,' said Deukalion. 'I worked that out to get us back here.'

'Here,' said Pandrosos, pointing at but not touching the dot. 'An island just a bit north of here.'

'Where they can summon the creatures they bring here,' said Actaeus. 'The Doctor said he had fixed their magic.'

'He's up to something,' said Deukalion. 'He must be.'

'He didn't look like it,' said Aglauros.

'Well, he's not going to make it obvious,' said Deukalion. 'That is kind of the point.'

'Maybe,' said Actaeus. 'But you said we should fight back.'

'I didn't!' said Deukalion. 'We're not meant to fight! June said we can be smarter than that.'

'We don't need to fight them,' smiled the king. 'They have conjured fuel and oil and wine out of the air. We can just use their magic against them.'

'So what's the problem?' asked the Doctor, stepping into the arena with the cocktail-swilling aliens. June felt a thrill just at the sight of him. She ran over, throwing her arms round his shoulders.

'You're all right!' she said.

'I'm better than that,' he said, disentangling himself. 'And you've been pretty brilliant, too. I take it this is your idea?'

She felt herself flushing with glee. 'I had a hand in it,' she said.

'If only the humans had thought to back down in the real war!' he went on. 'Billions of lives would have been saved.'

June regarded him carefully and his smile faltered. 'Humans did something terrible, didn't they?' she asked.

He shrugged. 'I'm not really meant to tell you,' he said.

'Spoilers. You know how it is.'

'But enough to make all these creatures despise us. To want us written out of history.'

The Doctor looked round at the assembled alien creatures. 'Is that what you wanted?' he asked. The alien tourists looked down at their feet – those of them with feet. They murmured indistinctly and would not meet his eye.

'All right,' said the Doctor. 'But it's not what you want now.' The aliens looked up, eager to assure him that they'd seen the error of their ways.

'I never wanted it,' said Cecrops, slithering forward on his fishy tale. 'Sorry,' he went on. 'I just didn't want you lumping me in with the rest of this lot.'

The other tourists groaned. June saw the Doctor glance over at the three Slitheen, whispering to one another behind the tourists. Mamps looked up at her and smiled cruelly, showing razor-sharp teeth.

'No really,' Cecrops went on. 'The package tour is the only way you can get back to see this stuff. But most of the people who come on these things are...' He tailed off. 'Well, they don't take it as seriously as I do.'

'We've been discussing rights for humans,' June explained to the Doctor.

'Right,' he said.

'Human beings are people too,' added Cecrops. A murmur went through the crowd at this. Cecrops turned on them, raising himself up to his full height. 'There's so many stories,' he said. 'About their greed and violence, the things they've done to other species. But is that any different from the rest of us?' He let them hang on that for just a minute, then came in with the punchline. 'Sounds just like my family.'

The tourists stared at him. And laughed. They turned to each other and began to compare amusing stories about the shocking things their own families had done. The Slitheen looked on in horror.

Cecrops turned back to the Doctor and June. 'Was that all right?' he said.

'Brilliant,' said the Doctor. 'You've got them looking for ways that we're all the same. Taking the initiative themselves.' He twisted round to look up at the stars, then looked back again. 'And just in time, as well.'

June went over to Cecrops. 'So you don't get on with your family?' she asked him.

He smiled sheepishly. 'They don't get on with me. Everything's got to be about how we're seen and what people think. Don't ask questions, don't cause a fuss. Certainly don't do anything political…' He looked round at the gabbling tourists, and then back to June. 'Whoops.'

But she hadn't stopped teasing him yet. 'So you're not here to change my world,' she said. 'You're just running away from your family.'

'I'm not,' he said, affronted. 'I just needed to clear my head. You know, work out my priorities.'

And she did know that need to get away. She could see the same restlessness in him that she felt herself. Just as he'd said, they weren't very different. She took a step towards him. 'When this is over—' she began.

'You'll be dead,' gurgled Leeb, striding purposefully towards them.

Cecrops bravely put himself between June and the Slitheen. But Leeb only giggled the more. 'Boy,' he said loudly, so everyone could hear. 'You're guilty of corporate espionage. We all heard you loud and clear.'

The alien tourists clucked at one another, trying to remember what had been said. June reached forward to take Cecrops' hand.

'I didn't say anything of the sort,' he told Leeb.

'You said you weren't part of the package deal,' Leeb crowed. 'Nobody takes it as seriously as you.'

The alien tourists decided that yes, Cecrops had indeed said those very words. They also remembered the way he'd set himself up above them. June saw the lion-faced couple with the huge wings nodding their heads together, their earlier differences forgotten now Cecrops was in the frame.

'I didn't mean it like that,' he protested.

'You're an *agitator*,' sneered Leeb. 'Corporate espionage is a very serious crime. It carries a very serious penalty.' He giggled. 'In fact, if we have reliable witnesses, we can choose any penalty we like.' His smile vanished as he turned to the alien tourists. 'And we have reliable witnesses, don't we?' he barked at them.

The alien tourists didn't mistake his tone. They murmured their assent.

'Good,' said Leeb. 'So now we're going to have a hunt. Mr Cecrops and the humans he's augmented to tell these lies. Versus anyone who'd care to join me.'

Cecrops and June backed away towards the Doctor as Leeb came slowly forward. The alien tourists exchanged nervous glances, not sure how to behave. Cosmo and Mamps emerged from between them, taking their places beside Leeb. One Slitheen each against Cecrops, the Doctor and June.

'Sorry,' said Cecrops. 'Said I shouldn't do anything political.'

'You were good,' June told him. She leant forward to kiss his cheek. Then she turned back to the Doctor. He was looking up at the sky.

'Um,' she said. He seemed startled as he looked round at her.

'What?' he said. 'Sorry, I wasn't paying attention.'

'They're going to kill us,' she said, indicating the three Slitheen. The Doctor looked up at them and grinned.

'No they're not,' he said.

Mamps laughed. 'And what's going to stop us this time?' she asked.

'You need me,' said the Doctor.

'What for?' asked Mamps.

The Doctor turned to June, a huge grin on his face, and then turned back to the Slitheen. 'Because I'm the only one who'll get you and your punters back home.'

Mamps froze. Just the look on her green face made June want to burst out laughing. 'What did you do?' said the Slitheen.

'When I said I was fixing the systems?' said the Doctor. 'Well, I was fixing the systems. First, I made it make a tunnel through time. One end open in the year Arlene-plus-22, the other open just twenty-four hours from now. Then I put a password on the end that opens up tomorrow, so only I can open it. And then I got the machine to transmat itself into orbit, just – ' he left a dramatic pause '– over there…'

With a flourish he pointed up at the stars. June, Cecrops, the Slitheen and the alien tourists all looked up where he was pointing. The blanket of stars remained unchanged.

After a moment the Doctor let his hand down, scrutinising the finger with which he'd pointed.

'That's odd,' he said. 'I thought there'd be a bang.'

'Another bluff,' preened Mamps, taking another step forward. 'You've run out of surprises.'

'Um,' said the Doctor, glancing at June. 'Yeah. Sorry, I thought that would work.'

'It's OK,' she told him, holding on to Cecrops. 'We gave it our best shot.'

And before the Doctor could reply, a voice sounded from high above them: 'I sing the last song of King Actaeus!'

They all turned to look. On the balcony looking down on the arena, on them, three tall silhouettes blanked out the stars. June gasped as she recognised them. Deukalion stood flanked by Aglauros and Pandrosos.

'It's the drunk human!' said Cosmo.

'What does he think he can do?' said Mamps.

'What's this all about?' the Doctor called up to him.

Deukalion smiled. 'You think we're stupid,' he said to the aliens. 'You bring us here to play your evil games and you think that we are helpless. But tonight we strike a blow for humanity.'

'Not another one,' moaned Mamps. Some of the aliens concurred.

'The final one,' Deukalion declared. 'The great King Actaeus gives his life for the people. The masters are masters no more!'

Mamps and the other Slitheen began to run towards the balcony, where Deukalion and the king's daughters stood firm. June felt a chill run through her as she turned to the Doctor.

'What can Actaeus do?' she asked.

The Doctor scratched at the back of his head. 'Well, nothing,' he said. 'I mean, even if you attacked the temporal drives with a sword...' His smiled faltered. He turned round, away from the Slitheen and the aliens and Deukalion, in the direction of the sea.

In time to see the whole sky erupt in flames.

SEVENTEEN

The fuel splashed slickly over the magic instruments and the metal floor, splashing against Deukalion's bare ankles. He had seen the masters cover a town in this stuff; flame consumed it quickly, water would not put it out. No one had escaped. Deukalion and a few others had been chosen at random to survive so that they might sing the tale to others. Those who dared oppose the masters met the most terrible ends.

He had tried to remind Actaeus and his daughters of this as they dragged crates of fuel through the magic portal that had brought them here from the citadel. But the old king would not heed the warnings. His people had been scattered into the hills, he had no kingdom or anything else left to lose.

Fuel dripped from the gantry down onto the machines below. Actaeus removed his cloak, dipped it into a crate of fuel, then threw it out over the balcony. He held on to one corner, so the soggy cloak snapped short, fuel spattering high across the cavern to slap all over the machines. Actaeus repeated the trick, fuel dripping thickly from the systems he had hit.

They worked quickly, unloading most of the fuel, then stacking the crates against the control bank of winking glass beads. Deukalion wanted to study the machine, to make sense of its awesome powers, but he knew this thing enslaved them. It let the masters bring ever more strange creatures here from the heavens – while it remained, people would live under their magic. It had to be destroyed.

'We are done,' said Actaeus at last. He hugged both of his daughters. 'Now,' he said. 'You must go.'

'We all go,' said Deukalion.

'No,' said Actaeus. 'One of us must stay to light the fire.'

Deukalion stared at him. 'You could light it, then press the map. Escape back to the citadel.'

The king smiled sadly. 'And perhaps in my haste it will not light. Deukalion, this must be done properly. I am proud to do it. Go.'

Deukalion protested, but Aglauros dragged him away. 'He is the king,' she said simply. 'We obey him in all things.'

Pandrosos hugged her father again and listened to his counsel. Then she joined Aglauros and Deukalion in the passageway leading back to the map. Actaeus stood proudly on the glistening gantry, his sword in his hand. He was smiling.

'We tell them,' said Pandrosos, 'and in his name, that the masters are masters no more,' she said.

'And then what?' asked Deukalion as they dragged him with them. 'We can't fight them!'

Pandrosos only smiled as they reach the map. She reached out and pressed the red dot that took them back to the citadel.

The sky danced with fire, purple and red and then, with a great roar of noise, the shockwave smashed through them, hurling them into the hot, dry sand. June lay there, stunned, looking up at the purple stars, wondering why no one was screaming. She realised with a start that she'd gone deaf.

Strong hands reached for her, helped her to her feet. Cecrops looked battered and bloody, but he was more concerned about her. She fought him off, knowing they needed to find the Doctor. It took a moment to spot him, up on the balcony overlooking the explosion. The three Slitheen stood beside him.

'Doctor!' she yelled as she ran for the steps and made her way round to him. Her voice sounded as if underwater and, though she said 'sorry' and 'excuse me' as she pushed through the alien tourists, they didn't seem to hear her. They gaped and cooed at the pretty colours of the sky, as if this were just another part of the evening's entertainment. But June knew better; something had gone terribly wrong.

The Doctor embraced her, holding her close. For a moment she thought he had been stunned into silence by the explosion. But as she withdrew from his arms she realised he was talking. She let him go, watching his lips as he gabbled on. He spoke too fast for her to pick out the words, his eyes wide with horror and amazement. The Slitheen kept close to him. They wouldn't kill him in front of the tourists – not without letting on there'd been some mistake – but they wouldn't let him escape.

'I can't hear anything,' she told them. But she had no idea how loud she had spoken and they didn't seem to register. So she shouted the same thing: 'Doctor, I can't hear!'

The Doctor turned his gaze upon her, still gabbling away. Behind her, Cecrops glided forward, eager to be of help. The alien tourists took pictures of the pretty sky. Ash and cinder rained down on them.

The Doctor tried asking June questions and she struggled to read his lips. Perhaps he mentioned a pineapple. Then he reached into his pocket for his sonic screwdriver and buzzed blue light into her ears.

Suddenly she could hear the whole awful night. The sky roared with fire and energy. The alien tourists twittered with excitement. 'They sure put on a good show,' she heard one enthuse.

'It's not good, is it?' June asked the Doctor.

'Keep your voice down,' hissed Mamps. She looked back at the alien tourists and said loudly, 'I'm glad it surprised you. We spent weeks planning it.'

The Doctor took June by the arm and led her further along the balcony, away from the tourists. Cecrops followed them, like a loyal dog.

'The temporal drives were built deep inside the rock,'

he said. 'The explosion must have taken out most of the island.' He shook his head sadly, an agonised look in his eyes. 'There would have been people living there.'

'Not any more,' said Cosmo, checking the readout of the bracelet on his wrist. 'I think the whole of Thera has gone. The temporal drive, the transmat... All of it destroyed.'

'Thera...' June repeated, trying to remember the word. It nagged at some part of her memory.

'Santorini,' said the Doctor. 'In your time, it's called Santorini.'

And June thought of the map she'd had for hopping islands on her holiday, a lifetime ago. An arc of land like the crusts from a slice of bread, the main body of the island lost beneath the sea. You could visit one of the towns buried in the ash... The ash only just falling now. June could almost hear the cries of the people out there across the sea. She gripped the Doctor tight.

'Cosmato,' said Mamps quietly. 'We need to send a signal to the family. Get them to send the time bus so we can get this lot home.'

'But without the temporal drive I'll have to build a relay,' protested Cosmo. 'That'll take for ever!'

'Then you'd best get started now,' Mamps glowered.

Cosmo thought better of protesting and hurried away.

Mamps turned to the Doctor. 'You see?' she said. 'We'll get this fixed. You've barely inconvenienced us.'

'I didn't do anything,' the Doctor told her. 'Well, nothing that would do anything like this. No, this is your own doing.'

'Hah!' laughed Mamps. 'How are we responsible?'

'You pushed the humans until they snapped,' said Cecrops. 'We tried to warn you.'

'The humans wouldn't know where to start,' said Mamps. 'They're three and a half thousand years away from discovering time-travel technology!'

'But they don't need to understand something to break it,' said the Doctor.

'Deukalion said it was Actaeus,' said June. She prodded Leeb in the arm. 'You were going to blow up his people.'

'What?' said Mamps. 'You didn't ask permission.'

'No!' protested Leeb. 'I just said I would. To make the prey behave!'

'Where is Deukalion?' asked Cecrops, looking round. June looked too, but Deukalion, Aglauros and Pandrosos had long since disappeared. So had the other human competitors. The Doctor caught June's eye, shook his head imperceptibly, telling her not to say anything.

'He'll be found,' said Leeb. 'And punished. I think we'll have a hunt.'

'It'd better be in the citadel,' said the Doctor. 'It's going to be a bit wet outside.'

They turned to look back over the citadel walls in the direction of the fiery sky. Mamps and Leeb both gasped, and it took a moment for June to realise why. The sea no longer twinkled away in the distance. Instead, pale sand stretched to the horizon, the tide out for miles and miles.

'What's happening?' asked June.

'There's going to be tidal wave,' said the Doctor calmly. He looked up at Mamps. 'Tell me there's a force field round the citadel,' he said.

'We didn't think there was any need,' said Mamps sadly.

'Oh well,' said the Doctor, clapping his hands together. 'I've got a couple of minutes to rig one up.' He beamed at the Slitheen for a moment, then grabbed June's hand and dashed off across the balcony.

'Go find Deukalion,' he told her once they were out of the Slitheen's hearing. 'Make sure he's not being stupid.'

'Right,' said June, letting him go. He disappeared off up the passageway.

She turned, pleased to see Cecrops slithering after her, glad for the protection he gave her. The courtyard and balconies showed alien tourists, still admiring the purple sky. But there were no other humans to be seen anywhere. She tried to think tactics, what her priorities would be in Deukalion's place. And it seemed quite obvious.

'Cecrops,' she said as he reached her. 'Where do they lock up the rest of the competitors?'

Cosmo stood in the map room, surrounded by torn-open machines. He gurgled with frustration as he tried to fuse wires together, then slapped the large box he had taken apart. The Doctor skidded in behind him.

Cosmo threw him an angry glance. 'I'm going as fast as I can,' he said. 'I don't need any help.'

'And you're doing very well,' said the Doctor coming to join him, squatting down amid the tangled mess of wires and components. 'Can't be easy without the temporal drive. What are you using for the power supply?'

Cosmo shrugged. 'The distress signal has its own reserve,' he said.

'I'm going to have to commandeer it,' the Doctor told him. 'Sorry, I need the power. Otherwise we're all going to get wet. There's this huge tidal wave on the way.'

Cosmo blinked at him but the Doctor had already started work, feverishly lashing the wires together, his sonic screwdriver buzzing. His natural authority made Cosmo hesitate before interrupting.

'But we have to send the distress signal,' said Cosmo. 'Or we'll be stuck here for ever.'

'It's all right,' the Doctor told him. 'I'll make sure you get home.'

Cosmo nodded. 'But Mamps will be cross if I don't do what she tells me.'

A thought struck the Doctor. He smiled at Cosmo and started patching two wires together that would short out the whole system. 'I'll tell you what,' he said. 'If there's any power left from the force field, you can have it back.'

Cosmo considered. 'But will a distress signal get through a force field?' he asked.

'If I rig it up right,' the Doctor told him, his fingers working quickly as he fused another component to his machine. 'We'll make it one way, so anything can get out but nothing can get in.'

'Ooh,' said Cosmo. 'That's clever.' He leaned in to examine the Doctor's handiwork and noticed the error he'd worked in. 'But you're doing it the wrong way round.'

'Am I?' said the Doctor, innocently. He let Cosmo take over. 'Tell you what,' he went on. 'You make that work and I'll get the distress signal working.'

***

June followed Cecrops into the dark corridor of the humans' quarters. They were more like stables than bedrooms, berths of wood stacked up together, lined with straw and rags. It stank of too many people squeezed into too small a place, with little concern for hygiene. But the place was empty, the cell doors hanging open, the locks broken on each one. June and Cecrops hurried on.

They emerged from the dark into a flat, open space, encircled by high walls. It looked like the exercise yard of a prison in a movie. For a moment, June felt as if she was in a film, as she watched a large group of people in their various historical costumes clustered at the centre, busy practising dance moves. She saw Herse, Polos and Vik, and several of the people who'd taken part in the re-enactment of the Platonic War. They waved at her, delighted she'd chosen to join them.

As June and Cecrops hurried over to them, June saw Deukalion directing. He had a *kylix* of wine in his hand.

'Hi,' he said grandly as he saw them coming.

June didn't know where to start. 'What are you doing?' she said.

'I'm going to sing a story,' said Deukalion proudly. 'This lot are going to make it look good.'

'But,' said June, perplexed, 'why?'

'Well,' said Deukalion. 'The masters are stuck here now. So we need to show them a good time. Instead of the games, we can have a party, feed them, sing them our stories.'

June gawped.

Ash drifted down onto the dancers, nestling in their hair. 'And who's daft idea was that?'

'Mine,' Deukalion beamed. 'It's much better than trying to drive the masters into the sea. That's what Aglauros and Pandrosos wanted to do. Not their fault; I think Actaeus ordered it. He didn't know about us all working together.'

Cecrops smiled. 'But you convinced them otherwise,' he said.

'We don't have any kings with us,' said Deukalion, 'so we had to make the decision ourselves. Everyone made their own decision, and we counted up the results.'

'You voted?' said June, amazed.

'Is that what it's called? It was pretty close, to be honest, but the majority said we should look after the masters rather than trying to kill them. Hence the dance routine. It's us working together.'

'It's very well organised,' agreed Cecrops. June thought he'd be wowed by a human eating a boiled egg.

'Yeah,' said Deukalion.

'Not all of you,' said June. 'Where are Aglauros and Pandrosos?'

Deukalion looked all round. 'Um,' he said. 'Sulking, I guess. Along with all the other people who wanted to go to war. I don't think they're really into the performing arts.'

June felt her heart turn over. She couldn't believe the two warrior princesses would ever surrender so easily. She turned to Cecrops. 'We've got to get back to the courtyard,' she told him. 'They're going to do something stupid.'

Around them, beyond the high walls looming over the yard, they heard a horrendous growl of noise.

EIGHTEEN

The Doctor and Cosmo walked out onto the balcony to a chorus of applause. Behind the alien tourists, far beyond the citadel walls, an enormous tidal wave surged over the coastline. White spray exploded high over the landscape, the trees and grassland lost under dark, fast-moving water.

The aliens hurried round the citadel walls to watch the flood seethe and gnash towards them. Cosmo cheered as a small clump of stone dwellings was entirely consumed. But then he saw the Doctor's dark expression and his grin faded from his face.

'We're going to be safe, aren't we?' he said.

'I think so,' said the Doctor quietly. 'We'll see. But there could have been tens of thousands of people in the path of that wave.'

'Yeah,' said Cosmo nervously. 'But *we're* going to be safe.'

They made their way to join the alien tourists at the wall. Dark water filled the landscape, still surging quickly their way. It picked over trees and shrubs, pooling in the valleys, filling them flat and then coming on. They saw sheep and goats hurrying from the deluge, trying to find high ground. But there was no high ground. The water surged around the hill of the citadel itself, rising up and up, licking the stone walls.

Cosmo giggled in terror as they joined Mamps and Leeb. But the Doctor looked confident as he watched the water reach up over the top of the wall. The Slitheen squealed together, then broke into a laugh. The water continued to rise past the top level of the wall. It didn't spill *over* the wall, it just kept rising high into the air, pressing against the invisible barrier. They soon looked out, as if through glass, into the murky swirl. Bits of rock and tree bumped up against the barrier and were then lost again in the gloom.

The alien tourists applauded and took pictures. Some brave souls reached hands or tentacles over the citadel walls. They could press through the barrier, touch the water, feel it warm and wet. But when they withdrew again, their hands and tentacles were dry.

The Doctor beamed. 'Yeah,' he told Cosmo. 'We're going to be safe.'

'You mean you weren't sure?' said Cosmo, appalled.

The Doctor grinned. 'Well, not a hundred per cent. But congratulations. You did that.'

Cosmo glanced back at the wall of water, already falling away, then at Mamps and Leeb. 'Yes,' he said proudly. 'So I did.'

'When the water dies away,' the Doctor told them sternly, 'we start getting the tourists out. You pack up and go home.'

'Do we now?' said Mamps.

'Yes, you do,' said the Doctor. 'Enough is enough. Too many people have died.'

'No one that matters,' said Mamps.

But before the Doctor could respond there was a cry from behind them.

The alien tourists gazed in horror over the citadel walls as the water fell back. Mamps ran forward to see what had appalled them. The flood had churned up the landscape, ripped out all the trees. Bodies of sheep and cows lay broken in the mud. What had been just a moment before a beautiful landscape now looked like a vision of hell.

One of the alien tourists began to take pictures, the bulb of the flash vivid in the night. A few others reached for their cameras, too, but they were all utterly silent as they took in the awful sight.

'The party's over,' said the Doctor. 'They'll tell their friends what you did.'

'But we didn't do anything!' said Mamps. She addressed the tourists. 'You know this wasn't us! It was that group of humans!'

The tourists shifted uncomfortably. One of the Balumin came forward, a pale blue creature with long tentacles painted in lurid tattoos. 'Yes,' it said, 'but only because of the way you'd been treating them.'

'You're just as bad as they are,' chipped in another alien.

'You're worse,' said a third. 'Imagine that! Worse than a human!'

The aliens twittered with horror at this revelation. Mamps and Leeb tried to placate them, but couldn't make themselves heard. The aliens demanded their money back and said they'd write to the news networks.

Mamps turned on the Doctor. 'You ruined everything!' she seethed.

'Whoops,' he told her, grinning.

'The humans are barbarians. They burned whole worlds in the Platonic Wars.'

'There were terrible things done on both sides,' said the Doctor sadly. 'And it doesn't mean you can wipe them from history.'

'But if we don't,' said Mamps, 'the humans wipe out the Slitheen.'

The Doctor blinked at her. 'Do they?' he said. 'Since when?'

'We've travelled in time,' Mamps pleaded. 'We've seen what gets done.'

'Well,' said the Doctor, 'I'm sure I can have a word. Humans are very amenable, if only you talk to them nicely.'

'Doctor!' yelled June. He turned and saw her and Cecrops heading towards him across the balcony.

'See?' he said. 'This is my friend June. She's nice.' Alien tourists crowded round, keen to meet her.

'Doctor,' said June, pressing her way through the crowd. 'Aglauros and Pandrosos. They're raising an army.'

'What?' said the Doctor.

The alien tourists muttered with fear at the idea of a human army.

'See?' crowed Mamps. 'And they took no prisoners in the Platonic War. A baaraddelskelliumfatrexius can't change its pustules.'

'But I told them *not* to fight!' the Doctor insisted. Then he stopped. 'A what?'

'A baaraddelskelliumfatrexius,' said Mamps. 'It's a beast on our home planet. Sort of like a giant squirrel. Extinct now, but they used to have pustules.'

'Yeah, I got that,' said the Doctor. 'Look, be fair, the humans do have a lot to be cross about. But I'll talk to them. Make this right.' He turned to June. 'Where are they?'

'We don't know,' June admitted.

'Over there,' said Cecrops.

They turned.

An army of humans had assembled in silence on the far side of the balcony, blocking their escape. The humans were dressed in the same daft historical clothes as before, but they'd added bits of armour, metal shin pads and boars' tusk helmets, where they'd been able to scrounge them. Those at the front carried tall, oblong shields, on which were painted the same crude logo – a human stick man back-flipping over a bull. The alien tourists huddled together in fear.

'Hey,' said the Doctor indignantly. 'That's me on those shields. You can't use me as your emblem if you're going to fight.'

One of the warriors stepped forward. Aglauros looked terrifying in her hotchpotch armour, a boars' tusk helmet wedged on her head. 'You showed us we could resist the masters,' she declared.

'But you weren't here for that bit,' he replied. 'I showed you not to fight.'

Aglauros shook her head sadly. 'The masters are masters no more,' she said. 'I promised my dead father.'

'Look, I'm sorry about Actaeus,' said the Doctor. 'But this really isn't the way…'

'If you're not with us,' said Aglauros, 'you're with them. And we have vowed to show them no mercy.'

'Now hang on just a moment—' began the Doctor.

'Oh, let them come,' gurgled Leeb. He and Mamps and Cosmo stepped forward to face the human army. 'I've not killed anything since this morning!'

'No,' said the Doctor. 'You've got this all wrong!'

But the humans were already charging.

NINETEEN

Leeb raised one claw at the humans racing towards him. He clicked the controls on the bracelet at his wrist, but the Doctor launched himself at the huge Slitheen, knocking his arm so that the death beam fired high over Aglauros' head.

Leeb struggled with the Doctor, trying to grab him. The Doctor couldn't escape, so he leapt right at Leeb. They both toppled over the balcony to crash down in the sand of the arena below.

The wave of humans broke on the alien tourists. Some of the aliens stood their ground, sweeping claws and tentacles at their attackers. Mamps and Cosmo were laughing as they waded through the human shield, warriors screaming as they were trampled and cut down.

'Doctor!' yelled June, running to the railing. The Doctor lay in the sand, unmoving. Leeb got unsteadily to his feet and raised his claws above the Doctor's head. June could do nothing – and then something moved suddenly beside her. Cecrops threw himself over the railing of the balcony to slap hard onto Leeb's back. They tumbled over in the sand and were up again quickly to face off against each other.

'You're dead, fish boy,' Leeb taunted.

Cecrops didn't say anything. Leeb charged, Cecrops rolled back on his tail and let Leeb smash into the wall of the arena.

June laughed, and ducked her head as a tentacle whipped towards her. A blobby creature fought a man with two swords, blocking and parrying as they danced back and forth. June struggled to get out of their way.

Half the alien tourists had joined the fight, the other half cowering behind them. June caught sight of Pandrosos duelling with Cosmo, her sword clattering against his claws.

'You've got to stop!' she shouted. 'We won't get anywhere like this!'

'Who's side are you on, girl?' growled a soldier in front of her.

'I'm not on anyone's side,' she insisted. 'There shouldn't even *be* any sides.'

No one listened. She ducked and weaved through the fighting, trying to get to the steps that led down to the arena. Her only hope, she felt sure, was to get to the Doctor. A human man cried out as Mamps slashed her claws through him. Then the great Slitheen turned on Aglauros, who dodged nimbly from the talons as they swept her way.

To June's horror, Aglauros and Mamps were both grinning, enjoying every moment of this.

She reached the stairs, clambering past a human soldier lying face down on the steps. June grabbed the banister and jumped over him, landing so hard in the sand that she lost her footing. Rolling forward, she missed a spear that thwacked into the ground where she'd stood. She looked up, around, but couldn't tell which of the tangled combatants had thrown it. Her bare feet ached but she had to keep moving.

Leeb and Cecrops circled round one another in the middle of the arena. The Doctor lay on the floor to one side and June hurried towards him. Leeb slashed at Cecrops, who hopped back, lifting himself on his hands and slapping the Slitheen hard in the face with his tail. Leeb fell backwards, flipped nimbly over and was back on his feet again.

June reached the Doctor, grabbing his shoulder to turn him over on his back. His face was covered in sand, which she tried to scrape away. Suddenly his eyes snapped open.

'Ow,' he said indignantly.

'You fell off the balcony,' she told him.

He sat up, waving her off. 'No, ow, you're rubbing sand in my face.'

'I was rubbing it off.'

'Oh,' he said. 'Oh, well, that's all right then. Good on you. What have I missed?'

'Everyone's gone mad,' she said as he looked all round. The Doctor got quickly to his feet, trying to work out where to start. Leeb slashed at Cecrops and just caught him on the arm. Cecrops yelled out in pain and toppled backwards.

Leeb leered, taking a step towards his fallen adversary. He reached for the bracelet on his wrist, the one that fired the death ray. And the bracelet wasn't there.

'Looking for this?' asked the Doctor. He held the bracelet in his hands.

'That's mine,' seethed Leeb. 'Give it here.'

'It's for molecular repurposing, isn't it?' said the Doctor, fiddling with the controls. 'You use it to turn sand into drinks and nibbles.'

'Give it here,' Leeb insisted, swiping at the Doctor, who ducked quickly out of the way.

'I just want a go,' said the Doctor. He grinned. 'All this physical exercise,' he said. 'Doesn't it make you hungry?' Before Leeb could respond, he aimed the bracelet at the sand and pressed the little button.

The sand exploded with pink light just in front of Leeb. He cried out as objects smashed into his legs and belly. Cakes and biscuits slapped against him, knocking him backwards a step at a time. The more he retreated, the more the cakes and biscuits came.

'Waaah!' he wailed, protecting his face with his claws. Biscuits smacked his shoulders. He hit the back wall of the arena and still the biscuits came. Leeb fell on his knees, sobbing, and was quickly buried under a cairn of cakes.

'You killed him,' said Cecrops in amazement, getting up off the ground.

'Nah,' said the Doctor. 'Just pinned him down for a bit. Taken him out of the game.'

'But those are just cakes,' said June.

'Rock cakes,' said the Doctor. 'Heaviest thing I could think of. Come on. We've got to stop everyone else.'

Bodies blocked their way up the steps, so the Doctor got Cecrops and June to put their arms round him and pointed the bracelet at the sand at their feet. They rocketed up on a spire of rock cakes and pink steam, taking some of the fighters by surprise. June felt a mile high as she, Cecrops and the Doctor leapt from the spire down onto the balcony. The balcony felt sticky under her bare feet. Aliens and humans stopped to stare.

The Doctor took the opportunity to step neatly between Mamps and Aglauros, grabbing Aglauros' sword out of her hand. He held the sword in one hand and raised the bracelet in the other. Mamps took a swipe at him but he dodged easily out of the way.

'Now, now,' he chided. 'This bracelet does funny things to sand. I wonder what it could do to a silicon-based life form.'

Mamps stared at him, wide-eyed. 'You wouldn't,' she said.

'Maybe you shouldn't force me,' he said. 'I thought we could have a natter. Oi,' he shouted at the rest of the fighters. 'Time out, if you please!'

Around them, June saw the fighting stop as humans and tourists turned to watch the stand-off between the two leaders. A lion-faced man with wings like an eagle's even let the human women he'd been fighting step round him for a better view.

'Right,' said the Doctor. 'Aglauros. Hello, that's a pretty outfit. Tell Mamps here that you're sorry.'

'What?' said Aglauros in horror. 'I would rather die.'

'I'd be happy to oblige,' gurgled Mamps.

'Oh,' said the Doctor, surprised. 'Really? They're not masters any more. I thought that's what you wanted.'

'We want all the masters dead,' said Aglauros. And she drew a dagger from a scabbard at her waist and lunged at the Doctor.

He parried with the sword he'd taken from her, but Aglauros twisted round and slashed at him again. The Doctor dodged, bumping into Mamps. 'Sorry,' he said as he blocked another attack from Aglauros.

'Don't mention it,' grinned Mamps. 'Let me know if I can be of any assistance.'

'Oh, I'm fine,' said the Doctor as he and Aglauros slashed and parried their way through the aliens and soldiers. 'But this is stupid!' said the Doctor as they went.

Aglauros snarled at him. 'Death to the masters!' she shouted. 'Death to those who help the masters!'

To June's horror, Aglauros' army took up the shout, turning again on the alien tourists. Battle resumed, more bitterly than before. A lumbering alien crashed into June as it dodged round a man with a spear. She recovered herself in time to see Cecrops, backed up against the wall by Pandrosos.

'Death to the masters,' Pandrosos told him.

'But I'm really into human beings,' Cecrops tried to tell her.

June cried out as Pandrosos lunged her sword at

Cecrops. There was a metallic clang.

'Sorry,' said Deukalion, holding Pandrosos' sword back with his own. 'He's with me. Got a problem with that?'

Pandrosos stepped back, twisted round and slashed at him. Deukalion blocked her without even trying. He held his sword in one hand, Pandrosos gripped hers in two. Their swords slashed and clacked and clanged as Deukalion kept her from Cecrops.

'You're on the wrong side!' Pandrosos seethed.

'You're attacking people who don't even have weapons,' said Deukalion. 'That just isn't fair.'

Cecrops escaped from behind Deukalion and slithered quickly over to June. 'Look,' he said. She turned to see Herse and Polos protecting the lion-faced man from two human soldiers. The lion-faced man seemed even more appalled to be rescued by humans than attacked by them.

Across the balcony, the Doctor and Aglauros continued to duel. The Doctor leapt for the tall spire of rock cakes, skidding down the side to land in the arena. Aglauros was hot on his heels. They danced over the sand, cutting and thrusting, neither finding an advantage.

Humans and alien tourists still clashed swords and talons up on the balcony. But Deukalion's friends were slowly getting between them.

Two of them even guarded Mamps. June saw her shake her huge head in exasperation.

'I was enjoying that,' Mamps opined to Cosmo. 'Why do we all have to be so rational?'

Then she gestured for Cosmo to come closer, whispering something in his ear. June nudged Cecrops and they both ducked round the various soldiers to follow Cosmo as he hurried away.

They left the quieting battle as Cosmo charged down one of the corridors and into the strange labyrinth of guest rooms. He ducked round a corner ahead of them and they hurried to keep up.

'We can't lose him,' June said. 'He can't be up to anything good.'

The passageways jutted off at sharp angles and split off in all directions. They sometimes lost sight of Cosmo for a moment as he took a sudden turning. He and Cecrops could both outrun a human and June soon had a stitch.

They lost sight of Cosmo just before a junction of three possible paths. Cecrops listened carefully, but they couldn't tell which way Cosmo might have taken.

'Split up?' said June.

'You can't face him on your own,' said Cecrops.

'Don't worry,' she said, 'I'll scream if I need you.'

Before he could argue, she ran off down the right passage. She glanced back to see him taking the left.

She hurried up the gloomy passage, listening for any movement ahead. Round a corner, she found a long corridor of doors. Curtains shrouded each of the openings. The corridor ended in a wall, so she didn't have much choice. She ran to the first of the doorways and poked her head round the curtain.

A large, square bed filled most of the room. At least, she assumed it was a bed. It might also have been some kind of bath, filled with idly wriggling spaghetti. There was no sign of the Slitheen.

June checked the next room and found an identical bed. Clothes lay scattered all round the floor, with a heap of dirty whites in the corner.

She had checked four rooms when she heard Cecrops cry out. 'June!'

She fled back up the passageway in time to see Cosmo emerge from the one on the left. He had something bundled up in his claws, and when he saw her, his eyes opened wide. With a high, mewling cry he sprinted away from her, back up the way they had come.

June didn't follow him at first. 'Cecrops?' she called up the left passageway. 'Cecrops, are you OK?'

She didn't get an answer.

With a thrill of horror she started forward. 'Cecrops, it's OK. I'm coming!'

She followed the passageway round to an identical corridor of doorways. One curtain had been slashed through, the long stripes of material flapping sadly down. Terrified of what she would find, she ran into the room.

Cecrops lay sprawled in the bed of slowly wriggling worms. Three lines of red streaked down his shoulder and chest where Cosmo must have slashed him. He winced as the wriggling worm in his hand nosed around the first of the wounds. And when he opened his eyes he saw June.

'What are you thinking?' he said to her. 'Get after him, quick!'

'Right,' she said, too stunned to argue, and turned tail back out into the passageway. She ran, struggling to remember the route they had come in by, unable to stop to work it out. She felt stupid for not having paid more attention, and for the rage coursing through her at Cecrops. How dare he snap at her when she'd been making sure he was all right.

Then, for a moment, she thought she'd got herself lost. The passageway didn't mean anything to her. But again there came that strange, high-pitched wail, up ahead of her. She redoubled her pace.

The passageway twisted once more and then she recognised the corridor that led into the arena. Cosmo skulked up ahead, cuddling whatever he'd stolen, just by the entrance to the arena. June tiptoed up behind him, but he glanced back to look at her.

'You can't jump out on me,' he giggled at her. 'I could smell you from more than a mile away!'

June stopped, instinctively sniffing to see what stink she gave off. Cosmo giggled and turned away from her. He bent, letting go of the bundle he'd been holding so carefully. Something lumpy fell out onto the ground, letting out a high-pitched wail as it fell. June ran forward to see as the thing landed with a bump on the floor. It sat for a moment, looking up at Cosmo in shock, and then let out a terrible cry.

'Mummy!' it wailed as June ran towards it. A little, lion-like face turned away from her, and it hurried away on four stumpy legs. The stumps of its nascent eagle wings waggled as it ran.

'Aw,' drooled Cosmo as it scurried away, 'you scared the poor little thing.'

He and June watched the little creature run out into the arena, past the pile of cakes and biscuits under which Leeb still lay. The Doctor and Aglauros still fought in the arena, their dance a little slower, more exhausted, but their skill still evident in every move.

Above them, the alien tourists and humans let out a shared gasp of surprise. They seemed to have finished fighting each other and crowded round the railing to watch the Doctor and the princess. Aglauros turned to see the little creature hurrying towards her.

'My baby!' cried a woman's voice from up on the balcony. And Aglauros dropped her dagger, running forward to snatch up the creature. June ran forward, out into the arena. The Doctor looked horrified and threw down his sword.

'All right,' he said, his arms out in submission. 'I surrender. Please, let it go.'

'My baby!' wailed the woman on the balcony – the lion-faced woman June had spotted before. Her lion-faced partner hammered the railing.

'Let him go!' he yelled at Aglauros. 'Wretched human! Let my son go.'

Aglauros twirled round in the sand, a wicked smile on her face. The watching aliens and humans gazed on in wonder, terrified of what she might do. June hurried towards the woman and child, but the Doctor raised a hand to make her keep her distance.

'Please,' he said gently to Aglauros. 'Look at him, he's just a child.'

Aglauros sneered at him without looking down. Then she yelled up at those watching above her.

'I had a child!' she told them. 'And my child had a father.

But the Slitheen killed them.'

The watching audience gasped in horror. The lion-faced woman let out a cry.

'They've taken everything,' Aglauros went on, her voice wavering with grief. 'The city I lived in, the king I obeyed, his people scattered in the wind. I have heard what you do in this citadel. We fight and die for your pleasure.'

The aliens looked shame-faced, but June saw Mamps grinning with pleasure. She realised anything Aglauros did now gave the Slitheen free licence to wipe out all the humans. They'd argue they had no other choice – like putting down violent dogs.

'Please,' said the Doctor to Aglauros. 'Don't do this.'

'No,' said June. 'Do.'

Aglauros snapped round to stare at her. She had a hand round the small creature's throat. The Doctor didn't dare get any nearer to her. But June took another step forward.

'You're right,' she told the princess. 'They've enslaved us for years. They've ground us down to almost nothing. They want to wipe us out.'

'Yes,' said Aglauros. But June could see the doubt in her eyes. The moment June had agreed with her, not given her something to fight, Aglauros was on the back foot.

'You want to hurt them back,' said June. 'It's not enough to stop them. They have to understand what they've done to you.'

'They need to know,' Aglauros agreed.

'And you know how much it hurts,' June went on.

'Yes,' said Aglauros.

'You can make them feel like that,' said June. 'You can

put that on them.'

The lion-faced man cried out in rage and frustration, a terrible, animal yell.

'But you're not going to,' said June. 'Are you?'

Aglauros looked down at the lion-faced creature for the first time. The alien creature wriggled in her grasp, then looked back up at her with wide, lion-like eyes. Aglauros gazed back, then looked slowly up at June. 'We could use him,' she said quietly. 'We could bargain with them.'

'You could,' said June. 'Are you going to?'

The lion-faced woman jumped over the railing, her wings unfolding to slow her fall. She landed lightly on the sand and walked slowly over. Tears cut tracks down her hairy face and her eyes were terrible to see.

'Please,' she said pitifully.

Aglauros reached out the child towards her without a word.

The lion-faced baby threw his arms round his mum's neck. The mother held him tight, gazing at Aglauros. Aglauros gazed back. June saw the desolation on her face.

'Thank you,' choked the lion-faced woman.

And above them, as one, the humans and alien tourists applauded.

TWENTY

'You're clearly more civilised than us,' the lion-faced woman told June.

'They have their moments,' the Doctor agreed, with a massive grin. He clapped June on the shoulder. 'That was brilliant,' he told her.

'It was awful,' she said. 'The poor woman.'

They watched Aglauros hanging from Pandrosos, sobbing together. Humans and aliens had come down from the balcony to join them in the arena. But they kept their distance from the two princesses, glancing awkwardly round at one another.

Cecrops eventually approached them. Pandrosos nudged Aglauros who looked up at the merman. He smiled sadly at her. 'If there's anything we can do,' he said.

She saw the scars on his chest from where Cosmo had slashed at him. 'You fought on our side.'

Cecrops smiled. 'There aren't any sides now.'

'Rubbish!' screamed Mamps hurrying over. She and Cosmo had used their bracelets to turn the cairn of cakes and biscuits back into ordinary sand. Cosmo now slapped Leeb around the face, trying to revive him. 'You kidnapped that baby!' Mamps went on. 'You were going to kill it!'

The Doctor made to protest. But the lion-faced woman stepped out in front of him.

'How dare you!' she said. 'This has all been your fault! You told us the humans were all willing volunteers! You said your tours were fair trade!'

'Yeah!' jeered some of the other aliens.

'Now, madam,' began Mamps as the tourists circled around her. Mamps stepped back and they surged forward. She turned to Cosmo, who'd got a dazed Leeb on his feet.

'Run!' she shouted, throwing her claws up above her head. But there were humans and tourists all round them.

'You're not going anywhere,' said Herse.

'Get out of my way, little ape,' Mamps crowed. 'I can still tear you in half.'

'You're not going to kill all of us,' said Herse.

A tentacled alien prodded Mamps in the arm. 'You're going to give us our money back.'

Mamps hissed at the terrible words. She turned to Cosmo and Leeb. 'Busted,' she said to them. And clacked a talon against the bracelet on her wrist.

Before anyone could stop them, Leeb had thrown his arms around Cosmo as he too worked his bracelet. Sand whirled up around the three Slitheen, sparkling with pink light. The aliens and humans fell back as the two pink clouds suddenly exploded with energy. And then there was no sign of the Slitheen.

'They blew themselves up,' said Cecrops.

'Not likely,' said the Doctor. 'They just repurposed themselves. Slitheen are made of silicon, like most of the sand. I expect they'll just revaporate somewhere else nearby.' He paused. 'Is "revaporate" even a word?'

'We've got to find them!' said June.

'Nearby as in anywhere in fifty miles. They'll keep their distance from the tourists, I think. Lie low for a while until their siblings turn up in the time bus.'

'Cosmo sent that distress signal,' said June. 'Why haven't they arrived?'

'Um,' said the Doctor. 'I sort of got in the way of the signal.'

'You stopped it?'

'No,' he said. 'I just sent it to someone else. Called in the alien hunters.'

'The who?'

The Doctor grinned. 'You and me. It's the signal we picked up in the first place.'

She gaped at him. 'And that time storm we crashed into, that was their temporal drive exploding,' she said.

'Yeah,' said the Doctor. 'Very good. You're getting the hang of this stuff.'

'So what will happen to the Slitheen if they're not rescued?'

'Oh, they will be,' said the Doctor. 'The family in the future will realise something's up. So they'll send the time bus back anyway.'

'You seem very sure of it,' she said, puzzled.

'Well, if they don't I'll give them a nudge. But first things first. Let's sort out how we're going to get these people home.'

The Doctor and Deukalion led everyone down the dark tunnel that led back to the tiny strip of beach. Humans helped alien tourists with their luggage and souvenirs, singing and chatting and teasing each other as they went. A couple of competitors from the kingdom of Mycenae were going to stay to look over the citadel. Everyone else couldn't wait to get clear of the place.

The huge *Cutty Sark* sat quietly in the cave where June and the others had first seen it. Some of the alien tourists admitted they'd been out on it before, but no one seemed sure how to pilot the thing, or how to get it out of the cave.

'It can't be that hard,' said the Doctor, buzzing his sonic screwdriver at a hatch in the wooden side. A gangplank slapped down in front of the Doctor's feet, leading into the ship's dark stomach. 'I mean, the Slitheen managed, didn't they? And I'm a lot smarter than them. Right, everyone aboard.'

The aliens and tourists trooped onto the ship, the gangplank wide enough for them to go in pairs.

'You can leave your swords behind,' he told Aglauros sternly. She snorted at him, looked ready to argue, then glanced round at her fellow passengers.

'We're all friends together,' she said.

'Exactly,' said the Doctor.

Aglauros unstrapped her daggers and dumped them in a heap beside the gangplank. The other humans and tourists dropped their weapons behind her

June helped the lion-faced woman carry her wriggling son on board. Her name was Amber but she looked puzzled when June asked the name of the boy. 'He's not really old enough to decide something like that,' said Amber. 'Though he is very smart for his age.'

They stepped onto the gangplank. The ship swayed and creaked in front of them, a huge yacht with vast, billowing sails.

Once everyone was aboard, the Doctor and June made their way up to the deck, already heaving with aliens and humans. There were incongruous, futuristic controls and the Doctor fluttered his fingers over them gleefully. Ahead of them, the cave wall just faded away. The morning sky and sea were streaked with red and purple, fallout from the explosion. It made for the most incredible sunrise. The *Cutty Sark* drifted effortlessly out into it.

Deukalion joined them at the desk of controls as the Doctor started the engines. It took June a moment to realise they were moving, the workings so smooth and silent. But the cliff face beside them began to slide by and then they were haring over the sea. The Doctor explained the simple controls to Deukalion who took great pride in taking the wheel.

'But can't we just teleport over?' asked June, pointing to the map on the wall. A red dot was casting out from the island of Crete, moving steadily northwards. 'That's us, isn't it? This ship has a teleport thing.'

'Yes,' said the Doctor. 'But where we're going doesn't. We'll have to go the long way. Come on, it'll be fun.'

June followed the Doctor out onto the deck again. Their fellow passengers had found a kiosk of tacky souvenirs – the same Greek heads and masks and athletes you could buy in June's own time, only made from stone. The Doctor used Leeb's bracelet to turn a box of broken statues into an ice cream stand. He and June began handing out cones and explaining to the passengers how they worked. June handed an ice cream to Cecrops, but he barely acknowledged her, staring out to sea.

'You all right?' she asked. 'Ready to go home?'

He smiled sadly but didn't answer.

A cry went up from the starboard side after they'd been going about half an hour. The Doctor ran round to look over the rails, then dashed to join Deukalion at the controls. Between them they brought the *Cutty Sark* round sharply. June hurried downstairs to join Herse and Polos unfastening the gangplank. They lowered ropes out of the wide door in the side of the ship, aliens coming to help them as they worked.

Then Polos scampered out, down the rope. June ran to the doorway to see him balanced on a makeshift raft. Two men, three women, a number of children and goats all gazed up at her, grinning. They had barely survived the previous day's flood, but they were not the only survivors.

With the Doctor and Deukalion at the wheel, the ship continued to pick up stragglers for the rest of the day. The aliens and humans already aboard fussed round, offering food and drink and explanations for all that had happened.

June kept by the doorway, working ropes back and forth, laughing as the stories being told got warped and exaggerated with each telling. At one point, she too had danced over the back of the bull in the arena. In another version the humans and aliens had put the Slitheen to the sword. The newcomers seemed to prefer the more violent versions.

They had rescued more than a hundred people as the ruin of Thera appeared on the horizon. June joined the crowd up on deck to see the awful sight. Two long, slender bread crusts of land marked the ends of what had once been a huge island. There was nothing between them now but darkly steaming sea.

Deukalion steered the ship expertly into a cove, under the Doctor's direction. He showed them which button lowered the anchor and the ship came to a standstill. They crowded round the deck to observe the dark, steaming crust of land. The contours had been smoothed by layers and layers of ash. There was no sign of life at all.

'We can't go out there,' said June. 'It must still be boiling hot.'

The Doctor grinned at her. 'The temporal drive was in the middle of the island. Much higher than anything that's left. We need to get up to the height of where the gantry would have been.' He licked his finger and held it out over the rail running round the deck. 'It's coming,' he said. 'I can feel the rent in time.'

He rummaged in his pocket to produce Leeb's bracelet, and fired it at the island of ash. Pink cloud whirled all over the island, rising high into the purple sky.

'What are you doing?' said June. 'You can't make a staircase out of food.'

'No,' said the Doctor. 'But I can absorb all the heat from the lava. Otherwise it'd be too hot for us to land there. And we've got a lot of work to do by this afternoon.'

TWENTY-ONE

They took everything they could from the *Cutty Sark*. They cut the masts down, they carried out all the furniture and fittings. They took boards from the floors and panels from the walls.

On the highest point of the strange, grey island, they worked together to construct everything they'd taken into a single plank, like a mile-long diving board. As the afternoon wore on, Cecrops led a team tearing up the ship's sails. They snaked the cord round and round the diving board tightly, so it acted like a handhold. It was the best they could do, but it didn't look very safe. June was glad she wouldn't be one of those to walk across this death trap.

Then the light was fading and the stars started to come out above their heads. Some of the alien tourists tried to spot their homes, pointing out constellations to the bemused humans. And then there was light in the sky across the water, high above their ship, in the space where the rest of the island had been.

'That's it!' shouted the Doctor. 'We haven't got long. We've got to get the gangplank out to it.'

They clustered round the huge long board they'd constructed and, from the sheer cliff face of the island, carefully fed it out into space to reach the rip in time. It was a tricky operation, steering the thing from one end, the weight ever greater the more they fed out into the air. The first time, they missed the rip in time completely and nearly dropped the board. But the Doctor spoke softly, encouraging them, and the second time they did it.

The far end of the board rested in the rip in time, as if hanging from a loop of string. Miles below, the sea lapped and splashed around the tiny *Cutty Sark*. The board seemed so fragile, so narrow, so high.

'OK,' said the Doctor, testing the cliff-side end of the board where it was wedged into the ground. 'It isn't open long. You've all got to get going.'

The alien tourists said their goodbyes and began lugging themselves and their luggage across the board. It bent under their weight and for a moment everyone held their breath. But the thing they had made was strong enough to take the weight of a few tourists at a time. The humans waved and cheered as the first tourist, a Balumin, walked down the diving board and vanished into the warped bit of space. A moment later he re-emerged. 'It works!' he said, grinning, and vanished once again.

The tourists streamed after him, laughing and waving

back down at the ship. But one tourist lagged behind the others. Then he stopped altogether.

'Come on, Cecrops,' said the Doctor. 'No dawdling. That tunnel won't last for long.'

Cecrops looked down at the Doctor and June. 'I've been thinking,' he said.

'Oh dear,' said the Doctor. 'That doesn't sound good.'

'I've been thinking how we stop this happening again,' he said.

Behind him, the lion-faced couple with the baby stopped and turned back round.

'Yes,' they said. 'We've got to make sure humans are left in peace.'

'What do you want to do?' asked the Doctor.

'I should die,' said Cecrops. He turned to the lion-faced couple. 'Tell my family I died, that the Slitheen did something wrong,' he told them. 'They'll sue the business for everything it's got. No one will ever try this again after my family are finished.'

'You can't stay behind,' the Doctor told him.

'Why not?' said Cecrops. 'There's nothing for me back home. I came here to escape all of that.'

'You'll be stuck here for the rest of your life,' said the Doctor.

'I know,' he said.

'You can't run away from things for ever,' June told him. 'Tell him, Doctor.'

The Doctor scrutinised Cecrops. 'You're not going to be told, are you?'

'No,' said Cecrops. 'And it's my decision.'

'If you're sure,' said the Doctor.

'I am,' nodded Cecrops. He looked up at the lion-faced couple. 'Please. Tell them it was the Slitheen's fault.'

The lion-faced woman nodded and took her partner's hand. They hurried up the steps and were lost in the warp of time. There were no more tourists left. The spindly board hung high in the night sky, one end in the swirling rip of time.

'But what will you do with yourself?' said the Doctor as he and June led Cecrops back down the slope towards the ship.

'I don't know,' said Cecrops, grinning. 'I'll find someone to take me in.'

He looked up at the humans gathered round the deck watching him. Aglauros smiled back at him. June felt a terrible pang of jealousy, but bit it down. Of course it made sense for Cecrops to stay behind. But the same wasn't true for herself. For the first time since she had met the Doctor, she longed to get back home.

'So it's finished,' she said to the Doctor. 'His family take the Slitheen to court and bankrupt the business. They never come back here again.'

'Yeah,' said the Doctor.

'So history's back on track.'

'Yeah,' said the Doctor.

'So why don't you look happy?'

The Doctor shrugged at her. 'There's still some loose ends. I mean, there's still the small matter of—'

A cry went up from the far side of the deck. They turned in time to see a man flying backwards through the air. June gasped in horror. The humans fell back from Mamps, Leeb and Cosmo.

'Hello again,' gurgled Mamps.

'They must have teleported aboard,' said June.

'We knew you wouldn't leave the tourists stuck in this backwater,' said Mamps. 'We can use your tunnel to get home.'

The Doctor nodded back up the slope of the island. 'You'd better get a move on,' he said. 'It's not going to be there for long.'

Mamps grinned. 'We have a few things to take care of, first,' she said. 'We're going to teach you apes a lesson. Now there's no wet-hearted punters to see.'

'There's no need for that,' said the Doctor. 'Just go.'

'Make me,' grinned Mamps, and she idly swept her talons out and killed one of the humans stood by her side. The man toppled back, and those around him scattered in terror. Leeb and Cosmo chased after them, laughing.

'Stop this!' shouted the Doctor. 'You don't need to do this!'

'And you made us give up our swords,' shouted Aglauros.

'I wanted to avoid any fighting!' the Doctor protested.

The Slitheen tore through the humans, talons snickering with speed. Mamps launched herself at the Doctor. June grabbed him, hauling him out of the way just in time. Mamps crashed down onto the deck, springing round to attack them again. June tried to drag the Doctor away, but he shook her off.

'No more running,' he said.

Mamps loomed towards him, claws raised for the kill. The Doctor let her come. Mamps was seething with anger.

'That doesn't sound good,' the Doctor told her. 'I think you're getting old.'

'I am not,' she wheezed, looming over him. The Doctor grinned at June.

'When Slitheen get old,' he said, 'they suffer from hardening of their soft tissues. Slows them right down.'

'Like hardening of the arteries?' asked June. 'I think my granddad had that.'

'A bit like that,' said the Doctor. 'They slowly lose the moisture inside themselves. Bet it's uncomfortable.'

'I'll have you know,' said Mamps, bearing down on him, 'that I'm in the prime of life. I'm certainly quicker than you.'

She slashed her claws down on him. The Doctor ducked nimbly forward to grab her arm, but Mamps was too quick and tossed him casually aside. June saw the Doctor smash hard into the deck. Then she was looking up at Mamps's razor-sharp teeth.

'No one to save you now,' Mamps gurgled.

She raised her claws to strike. June cowered, nowhere to turn.

'I wouldn't,' said the Doctor, behind Mamps.

Mamps hesitated. 'And how are you going to stop me?'

'With your bracelet,' said the Doctor. 'I'm feeling rather peckish.'

June and Mamps both glanced at Mamps's wrist. The Doctor had swiped the bracelet when he'd grabbed her arm. Mamps turned slowly round. The Doctor aimed the bracelet in her direction. He took a step forward and pressed one of the buttons.

Mamps cried out, but nothing happened, at least not to her. Away across the deck, Cosmo, wrestling Cecrops, cried out as his own bracelet erupted in pink smoke.

'Go,' said the Doctor to Mamps. 'Before I change my mind.'

Mamps considered. Then she called out to Leeb and Cosmo. 'All right, that's enough. We're going.'

They retreated over the side of the deck and onto the island. High up the hill, the spindly diving board still reached out across the water to the rip in time. The humans kept their distance, tending their wounded and dead. June couldn't tell how many people the Slitheen had killed. But she seethed with anger at the dumb cruelty of it.

'You can't let them go,' she told the Doctor.

'Kill them,' said Aglauros.

'If they don't get back home, their siblings will come looking for them,' said the Doctor.

Mamps leered. 'They'll come in force.'

'You want the Slitheen to leave you in peace,' the Doctor told Aglauros. 'They will if you let these three go.'

Aglauros turned to look at the dead and wounded people, the awful things the Slitheen had just done. Then she nodded. 'Go,' she told the Slitheen.

'As you command,' Mamps snickered, starting up the slope. And then she leapt back down onto the deck.

She landed right in front of June. The shock knocked June from her feet. As she fell back, she saw Mamps withdrawing her claws. The Doctor cried out, running forward. Mamps laughed and leapt back to the island.

June lay back, stunned, watching the three Slitheen racing up the slope of the island, faster than the pursuing humans. Let them go, she wanted to say. But she couldn't get the words out. She looked down at her own body, at the gouge in her front where Mamps had stabbed her with one claw.

The Doctor and Cecrops were either side of her, talking quickly about what to do. Deukalion joined them, his eyes wide in horror. June felt no pain, just a bit woozy. Perhaps the Slitheen's claws were poisoned. Perhaps her own body had dulled the awful pain. She wanted to lie back and sleep. The Doctor yelled at her but she could barely hear him. She smiled to show she was OK, and fell back, her head hitting the deck as if it were a pillow.

As the Doctor and Cecrops fussed over her, she looked up at the diving board, reaching out into the night. The Slitheen stopped to turn back and slash their claws at the pursuing humans. She saw Polos dodge a savage blow. Then Cosmo threw his claws up and pointed to the rent in the sky. It shimmered with silvery light, straining to untwist.

The Slitheen turned away from the humans and hurried out across the diving board. It buckled and twanged under their weight. June saw them race across the diving board and hurl themselves at the rent in the air. And the rent just faded away.

Windmilling their claws and screaming, the three Slitheen dropped from the end of the diving board like stones. The board followed them, spinning round as it tumbled down into the sea. June lost sight of them behind the people fussing over her wound. The diving board had been maybe a mile high – no human could have survived such a fall. Despite what they'd done to her, she hoped the Slitheen survived. If they died, their siblings would surely enact a terrible revenge. She suddenly felt a terrible pain in her stomach, trying to consume her.

The Doctor gazed down on her, such agony in his eyes. His lips moved but she couldn't hear him. She struggled to read his lips.

'It's going to be OK,' he assured her.

She smiled, knowing he lied, and fell back into darkness.

TWENTY-TWO

June woke unable to move or see. She lay still, paralysed, staring up at the sweet-scented smoke curling above her, listening to the silence all around. Then she struggled to sit, but her arms were pinned to her sides by the blankets and her gut exploded with sudden, agonising pain. She fell back, letting out a single, ragged breath.

'It's OK,' said Cecrops, coming over to her and smiling. 'You're going to be OK.'

She smiled up at him, exhausted, then fell back into unconsciousness.

Later, they brought her outside on a throne of ornately carved black wood. Sunlight warmed her face and skin, made her feel alive. She sat high up on the rock that would one day be the Acropolis and let people fuss around her. Away in the distance she could just see the mastless ruin of the *Cutty Sark* moored in the bay. The tidal wave had hit here, too, the whole shallow valley covered over in dark mud. June knew she was getting better when she started to notice the smell.

But the mud proved very fertile, and June watched the Doctor wading about in it happily, followed by an entourage of the human soldiers. He had them cutting furrows and sowing seeds, all the time spouting enthusiasm and advice. Slowly the highly trained warriors learned the rudiments of farming. Herse and Polos were apparently the most gifted students.

'So they'll feed themselves,' she said to the Doctor one evening when he returned from his work.

He sat beside her in his mud-spattered suit, gazing out over the new allotments. 'We'll see,' he said. 'Now they know what they're doing, Deukalion will take people home in the ship. They'll spread the word, get everyone working...'

'But will it work?' asked June. 'Are people going to starve?'

The Doctor smiled sadly. 'It's not our problem any more,' he told her. 'There'll be more food here than they need for themselves. But this whole area is lacking in tin, which they need for making bronze. So they'll have to trade with other people.'

'So the different kingdoms work together,' said June.

'If they've got any sense. But you know what people are like. There'll be arguments and wars soon enough.'

June looked round at the people chatting and laughing, helping each other at the cooking fires.

'But it's not our problem any more,' she said softly.

'They have to do this for themselves,' the Doctor told her. 'No more interference. We can't wrap them in cotton wool.'

'So we're done here,' she said.

'As soon as you're feeling better,' he said. 'But yeah. Then we should be off.'

They held one last party up on the high rock. Cecrops dished out the wine, Aglauros and Pandrosos danced around the fire. They ate from wide clay bowls. The older bowls were painted with spindly octopuses and dolphins, but they'd also fired new pottery that showed an emblem of bulls' horns and a stick man flipping over a bull's back. It had become a symbol of their freedom.

Deukalion plucked at a five-stringed lyre and sang the story of their fight with the masters. The Doctor laughed when, in this version, it had been Deukalion's own idea to build the *Cutty Sark*. But June felt distant from it all, not sharing their excitement. Cecrops and the others assumed she still felt her wound and edged round her with care. But the Doctor leant in to whisper in her ear.

'Ready to go?' he asked.

'Yeah,' she said. 'It's harder the longer we leave it.'

He nodded. Then Cecrops grabbed the lyre and, a little unevenly, sang an old song from Earth's history, a pop song she sort of knew about a starman waiting in the sky. To the others' surprise, June sang along until the Doctor asked her to dance. Slowly, carefully so as not to strain her stitches, they zigzagged back and forth in front of the fire. June kept expecting to feel sudden pain, but it did not come. Deep down she knew she'd been well for days. She'd been stalling to stay just that bit longer…

They crept away before dawn, tiptoeing down the wooden steps from the rock and out through the door of the stockade. Moonlight glinted eerily over the new allotments, a breeze tickled at them as they ran. The Doctor held his sonic screwdriver out in front of them, ready for any lions.

'It's better this way,' he said. 'I've never liked goodbyes.'

But as June and the Doctor reached the TARDIS they found their friends waiting there.

'We couldn't let you just slip away,' said Aglauros, her arm round Cecrops' waist. June felt she could leave them to their lives now, could let them tell their stories, each time writing her and the Doctor out of history that little bit more. She felt even more itchy to leave them to get on with it.

'We wanted you to have something to remember us by,' said Deukalion. And he handed over a great amphora, painted with a somersaulting stick man.

'Thank you,' said the Doctor.

They variously shook hands and hugged. Cecrops sniffed back silvery tears.

'You'll be OK,' June told him.

'Yeah,' he said. 'And if the crops fail we've got that last bracelet. Magic up some supplies.'

'Not much juice in it,' the Doctor warned. 'You probably only get to use it once.'

'We'll be fine,' said Cecrops.

June leant up to kiss him on the cheek, then reached forward to whisper in his ear. 'Athens,' she said, 'made its money from trading olives and olive oil.'

He kissed her back. 'Good tip.'

'What was that?' asked the Doctor as she joined him at the door of the TARDIS.

'Nothing,' she said sweetly.

He scrutinised her for a moment then turned back to the others with a grin.

'Well, bye then,' he said. 'Best of luck.'

The Doctor closed the door and hurried to the dais of controls. Soon the great engines shuddered into life, the central column heaving with power.

'So we did it?' June asked him as he worked. 'History is back as it should be?'

'Oh yeah,' he said easily. 'With no more alien tourists, a new age is about to begin. One not of Gods and monsters but of extraordinary human beings. Your lot, the historians, call it the age of heroes.'

But something in his eyes disturbed her.

'You're sure?' she asked him. The Doctor didn't look round, his eyes fixed in concentration on the controls.

'Doctor?' she said, a chill going through her.

He shrugged. 'We'll go and see,' he said. 'Once I've found you a pair of shoes.'

TWENTY-THREE

The sun blazed down on them as they stepped from the TARDIS. June took the Doctor's hand and led him up the perfectly regular steps of the gleaming new theatre. Men in beards and simple tunics went about their business, not even sparing the two visitors a glance.

From the top of the theatre, in the shadow of the high rock, they could look back on the bustling city of Athens. Smoke curled from white, blocky buildings. There were temples and statues and all the noise of a busy community.

June marvelled at the sight. She'd studied this place, she had read all about it, and she almost felt she had been here before. Her eyes picked over the details: lines of clothes hung up to dry, children playing in the fields.

'It's not quite at its height,' the Doctor explained. 'But this is Athens booming. Its citizens living the good life.'

They made their way along the path leading round the rock. A pungent whiff reached them from the market down the hill. They could hear men in the market, making grand speeches, arguing philosophy and politics. June wanted to go and investigate but the Doctor held on to her arm.

'Let them work it out for themselves,' he said. She realised he'd heard her whispering to Cecrops.

'I only meant to help,' she said.

'It's cheating,' he told her. He glanced round. 'Funny,' he said. 'I can't see any women.'

June squinted. 'There's one, over there.'

Sure enough, there was a figure putting out some washing. She wore a shapeless all-in-one black outfit, covering her head and arms. 'Ancient Athenians had some funny ideas about women,' said June. 'The respectable ones wore the veil. It's funny, it makes it look more like something from the Middle East than the cradle of the West.'

The Doctor nodded. 'Women get the vote eventually,' he said.

'In Greece?' she said. 'You know when?'

'Um,' he said. 'No.'

'1952,' said June. 'You're on my turf now,' she laughed. 'I've studied this bit.'

'And what do you think?'

June stared at him. She struggled to find the right words. 'It's not what I expected,' she told him at last. 'I thought I would see it and then it would all make sense. But it's just as complicated and strange as before.'

'Yes,' he said, taking her hand. 'It's better than a lot of

other places from this period of history. And it's heading in the right sort of direction. But…'

'But,' said June, 'it could do better.'

'Yeah,' shrugged the Doctor. 'You don't like it?'

She grinned. 'I love it. Wouldn't want to live here. And it's still a bit of a shock. But I want a look at the Parthenon.'

'Done,' he said.

They continued round to the place which had once been a stockade, the entrance to the high rock. A soldier with a round shield and golden shin pads stood severely in their path. The Doctor fussed in his suit pocket and produced his wallet.

'Hello,' he told the soldier. 'We're come to inspect the Acropolis.'

The soldier nodded. 'Tourists, are you?'

'Er, yeah,' said the Doctor, surprised.

'Trade is our lifeblood,' the soldier explained. 'There's no fee, though we would ask you to remember the local gods on your way back out.'

'Right,' said the Doctor. 'Good tip. We will.'

The soldier took a step back, letting them pass. 'I hope you enjoy your stay.'

The Parthenon took a bit of getting used to. June and the Doctor boggled in front of the enormous temple, in the spot where future tourists would one day pose for photos. The roof and columns and all of it had been brightly painted in red and yellow and blue. The statues wore gaudy make-up, their bare skin brilliantly pink. June struggled to make sense of the sculptures running high above the columns. It took effort to pick out the details in all the sumptuous colour and paint work. But there, at last, she could see rows of horses marching in parade. She knew the procession of old, having seen the same stones, bereft of garish colour, in the British Museum.

'It's barking mad,' said June, gazing around in wonder.

'It looks like it's all as it should be,' said the Doctor.

A young man in a tunic came over to them. 'Hello,' he said. 'Have you visited Cecropia before?'

June blinked at him. 'Cecropia?' she said.

'Yes,' said the young man. 'Sorry, what do they call our city where you come from?'

Before June could respond the Doctor stepped in. 'It's got a few names,' he explained. 'But I thought you called it Athens.'

The man smiled. 'Yes, we sometimes call it that. Did you want a look at the goddess Athene?'

He led them inside the temple. Light stole into the dark space through specially made gaps in the ceiling. Scented smoke curled from braziers placed at regular intervals. June felt a thrill of excitement to be inside the incredible place.

Athene gazed down at them from an ornately carved pedestal at the end of the temple, a huge statue of ivory and gold. She stood tall, in a long tunic and breastplate, an elaborate boars' tusk helmet over her head, decorated in gold. In one hand she grasped a spear, in the other she held out a small, winged creature, as if offering it to those who looked on. June took a step forward to get a better look and gasped at the image painted on the goddess's breastplate.

'The gorgon Medusa,' their tour guide explained.

But June recognised only too well the green skin and black eyes.

'It's one of the Slitheen,' she said.

'Looks like it,' said the Doctor. 'Caught up in the history of the city, now. Part of the songs they sing.'

'Medusa turned people into stone,' said the tour guide, sticking to his script.

'I don't remember that bit,' said June.

'And then she saw her own reflection and turned to stone herself,' said the Doctor. 'Have you not seen *Clash of the Titans*?'

'No,' said June. 'I mean, yes, I've seen the film. But I don't remember the Slitheen turning anyone to stone.'

'Well,' said the Doctor. 'Stories can get mixed up together when you tell them for long enough. Have you not seen *Sherlock Holmes Versus the Titans*?'

June sighed. 'You made that up,' she said.

'Maybe I did,' said the Doctor. He turned to the tour guide. 'Tell us about Cecrops,' he said.

'Ah,' said the tour guide, pleased to show off his expertise. 'The first king of Athens. Half-man, half-serpent, he invented marriage and did away with blood sacrifice. He lived in a three-roomed house here on the Acropolis. And his daughters – Aglauros, Pandrosos and Herse – were turned to stone by the Medusa.'

'What?' said June, horrified.

'Well, that's one story,' said the guide quickly. 'It could have been Hermes that did it.'

The Doctor took June's hand. 'It's a thousand years

since we left them,' he told her. 'They were always going to be long dead.'

'How can you say that?' she said, tears tracking down her face. She felt awful for her earlier, stupid jealousy. 'After everything we've been through together, we left them to some terrible fate.'

'I'm sorry,' said the Doctor. 'But we don't know what really happened. It's just an old story now.'

Yes, thought June, desperate for anything to cling to. It was only a story. 'People don't get turned to stone in real life,' she said.

'No,' said the Doctor. 'That's silly.'

'Um,' said the tour guide. 'You can see them if you want.'

The Doctor turned to him. 'See who?' he said.

'The stone people,' said the tour guide. 'They're in a cavern under the Acropolis.' He grinned awkwardly. 'It's called the grotto of Aglauros.'

June insisted on seeing the grotto. They made their way back round the side of the Acropolis, past the theatre with the TARDIS on its stage, and into the wide-mouthed cavern where June had first rescued the Doctor, what seemed a lifetime before.

Their tour guide led them inside, bearing a flaming torch since electric light had not yet been invented. They passed statues and votive offerings – the guide explaining that the cavern attracted its own religious cult.

They emerged into an open space, three large figures looming out of the darkness. The Doctor and June approached them warily. Firelight danced over the bare stone – the statues had not been painted. They were expertly sculpted, life-size creations. June could see why people thought they had been living beings magically transformed into stone.

'The daughters of Cecrops,' said the tour guide reverently. 'At least, that's what the legends say.'

But June knew better. 'It's Mamps,' she said. 'And Leeb and Cosmo.'

'Yes,' said the Doctor, amazed. 'And pretty good likenesses, aren't they?'

But as they dared to get closer, the statues didn't look quite so perfect. The stone looked rough, as if the statues needed one more go with a chisel. June put out a hand to stroke the rough, glistening surface. She jumped as a droplet of water splashed down on the back of her hand. She looked up. A stalactite hung above her head. She dodged a second drip of water as it fell from the stone spike. The droplet spattered against Mamps's stone thigh.

She turned to the tour guide. 'Did you really think these things were princesses?' she asked him.

'Well,' he grinned at them. 'It's a good story, isn't it? Better than when they all live happily ever after.'

'You,' June told him, smiling, 'are such a boy.'

'OK,' said the Doctor, stepping back from the controls. 'Just as I promised. Back the moment we left.'

June felt cold, watching the controls, not wanting it to be over. 'Can't I stay?' she asked in a quiet voice.

'You'll miss your train home,' he told her, nodding at

the rucksack parked under a chair. 'And there are people waiting to see you.'

She nodded, reaching for the bag that contained so much of her old, real life. And felt a spasm of pain from the wound in her gut. Perhaps it was best that she left while still in one piece.

Something pinged on the dais of controls. The Doctor blinked in surprise and checked the instruments. Alien lettering scrolled across the screen.

'What does it say?' said June, coming over.

'Um,' said the Doctor. 'You remember those aliens trying to blow up the Acropolis?' he said.

'You called in the authorities,' said June. 'The space police.'

'Yeah,' said the Doctor. 'But it turns out those aliens are space police themselves.' He read over the message again. 'Investigating a case of tax fraud,' he said. 'But that doesn't make any sense. Why would they want to blow up the Acropolis?'

June considered. 'Maybe they weren't really blowing up the Acropolis,' she said. 'Maybe they were doing something else.'

The Doctor nodded slowly. 'They did say they had the best of reasons.' His eyes opened wide. 'Oh,' he said. 'Of course.'

He suddenly dashed across to the TARDIS doors and flung them open.

'What?' June called after him, but he'd already run out into the daylight. He called something back at her, but the only bit she caught was the word 'causality'.

June dumped the bag back under the chair and followed him.

June closed the door of the TARDIS and hurried up the ruined steps of the theatre after the Doctor. Above them, fat noisy tourists milled about on the top of the Acropolis, the same ones who'd asked her to take their pictures. June held her sore gut as she leapt up the uneven stairs, sweat beading on her brow.

The grotto seemed smaller than it had been just a moment before, two and half thousand years previously. Rocks crowded the gravel pathway as she hurried to catch up with the Doctor. She emerged into the open space where she'd first had to rescue him, but the Doctor was nowhere to be seen. Electric light shone brightly from the walls, but she still could not spy him.

Then he jumped out from beside the silver sphere that lurked behind the heap of explosives, piled high around three stalagmites. In his hands he held the wire with the tiny sphere hanging from the end.

'It's not a bomb,' he told June quickly, as he held the sphere between his fingers. 'Well, not as such. This thing focuses all the energy. It makes a lot of heat in a confined area, plus a few little chemical tricks.'

'Great,' said June. 'But should you be doing that?' The tiny sphere in his fingers had started to glow.

'Um,' said the Doctor. 'All I did was take off the lock that I'd put on it. It's doing everything else itself.'

With a start, he dropped the wire with the sphere on it, waggling his fingers in pain. The sphere steamed with energy, glowing brilliant pink. He glanced back at the larger sphere, banging his hand against it. Apart from the sound, it didn't do anything.

June grabbed the Doctor's arm and dragged him back from the high heap of sandbags. 'We've got to get out of here,' she said.

'Nah,' he said. 'It's not going to explode. Trust me. All that energy is being focused into the stones.'

The heap of sandbags began to shift with pink steam, and the stalagmites started to glow. June tried to drag the Doctor back from whatever was happening, but he looked on in fascination. Pink steam poured from the sandbags, enveloping the tall stones. Slowly the light faded from the tiny sphere and the pink steam dispersed into the air.

'Oh,' said the Doctor with disappointment. 'I thought it would be more exciting.'

He took a step forward and knocked his knuckles against the first of the stalagmites. The stone creaked like leather and then collapsed in small pieces, revealing the thing hidden inside.

Mamps stood there, her green flesh glistening wet, pink steam curling from her long talons.

'Thought so,' beamed the Doctor.

'They survived,' said June in horror.

'Oh yeah,' said the Doctor. 'Slitheen are pretty hard-wearing. They just calcified over time. Maybe they can do it on purpose, or it's just a sign of old age. But their soft tissues harden, mineral deposits build up. And slowly they turn to stone. Some enterprising soul thought they were statues and sent them to Athens, because it's hot on sculpture. And the Athenians thought they were ugly and stored them in the cellar. Something like that, I expect.'

'They were never rescued by their siblings,' said June.

'No,' said the Doctor. 'They've been stuck here for thousands of years. Buried under drips of limestone. Until we reversed the process.'

He tapped his knuckles on the other two stalagmites, which collapsed to reveal Cosmo and Leeb. They stood, eyes closed, not even breathing, pink steam curling from their wet flesh.

'Um,' said June. 'Do you think that's a good idea?'

'What?' said the Doctor. 'They're not going to be any trouble. And I've unlocked the space police, too. Not that they seem to have noticed. Oh well, they'll all be a bit slow and confused to begin with. Like anyone after a long sleep.'

But as he spoke the words, June saw Mamps's face twitch into a cruel smile. The Doctor turned to see, and Mamps's huge black eyes gazed back at him.

'Good morning,' said the Doctor, kindly.

'Yeah,' gurgled Mamps, sounding very awake. 'It will be.'

And she and the other two Slitheen pounced.

TWENTY-FOUR

The Doctor grabbed June just in time, yanking her out of the way of Mamps's claws. Mamps, Cosmo and Leeb smacked hard into the rock wall of the cave and fell back, stunned. For a moment, June thought they'd knocked themselves unconscious, but then they began to stir. The Doctor grabbed her hand.

'Quick,' he said. 'We don't have much of a head start.'

They ran hand in hand up the gravel pathway, out into the daylight. June felt a stab of pain in her guts, her stitches straining with the effort.

'What are we going to do?' she said.

'Easy,' said the Doctor, and then vanished in a green blur. He and Mamps tumbled down the ruins of the ancient theatre towards where the TARDIS stood waiting. The Doctor kicked and fought, giving as good as he got. Mamps wailed with surprise and pain.

June could do nothing to help. She turned to see Leeb and Cosmo emerging from the cave. They tottered uneasily, not fully awake. But when they spied her, Leeb smiled cruelly.

'Breakfast,' he gurgled.

June turned and ran as fast as she could, clutching her aching sides.

Leeb and Cosmo's footsteps slapped the dry ground behind her. June's first thought was to run down the theatre to the Doctor and the TARDIS, but Leeb leapt in front of her, blocking her path. She twisted, racing back up the ruined steps and following the path that led round the side of the Acropolis. Up above them, she heard the noisy tourists cry out at the strange sight. Then there came the clicks of cameras capturing the image of June running for her life.

She half-ran, half-slid down the steep path, unsteady in the shoes the Doctor had found her in some cupboard of the TARDIS. As she heaved her legs up the steep facing slope, she heard a crash behind her. Leeb and Cosmo had taken the hill with too much speed and come crashing down. She didn't stop, using the slight advantage to gain some distance.

Heart hammering, gut almost on fire, she staggered along the pathway and up past the ticket kiosk. The queue of customers stared at her in amazement as she ran past. As she caught sight of the good-looking guard on the gate, she heard the tourists scream out in terror behind her. And the gurgling delight of the Slitheen as they tore through the crowd.

The guard ran forward to help, but June grabbed his hand and dragged him through the gate and up the steps onto the high rock. 'What are those things?' he asked in horror, but she didn't have the breath left to answer.

At the top of the steps, she dared to glance back. The two Slitheen were still hard on her heels. Leeb leered up at her. 'There's no escape,' he said.

June let go of the guard's hand and sprinted round the side of the ruin of the Parthenon, her feet scrunching on the bright gravel. The noisy tourists parted around her, then screamed at the two Slitheen bearing down on them. June didn't look back, she raced to the far end of the Acropolis, where it looked down to the theatre.

The TARDIS stood there, just as she'd left it, tiny from so far above. But she could not see the Doctor or Mamps.

Gravel scrunched behind her and she turned to see Leeb and Cosmo trotting easily towards her. They extended their talons towards her, both wearing the same evil grin.

'You don't have to do this,' she told them, barely able to get the words out.

'You and your friend didn't have to ruin our business,' said Leeb.

'And anyway,' said Cosmo. 'We're hungry.'

He pounced. Leeb pounced too. And just before their talons touched her, June threw herself down onto the gravel. The Slitheen cried out, realising too late what she'd done. Leeb grabbed for the safety rail as he flew over it, but his great claws clattered on the metal and could not get purchase. He and Cosmo disappeared over the edge of the high rock with a wail of despair.

June struggled to her feet, her whole body aching. She carefully leant over the railing, just in time to see the two Slitheen smack into the steps of the theatre. They rolled clumsily down to the bottom, arms and legs waggling, crashing hard into the TARDIS. She watched them lying there, still on the stone floor, feeling nothing but horror. Her gut ached with the exertion, but her stitches remained in place. She needed to sit down.

Other tourists approached her, leaning over the railing to gaze down on the two Slitheen. June ignored their questions. She needed to see what had happened to the Doctor. But as she stood up again the tourists cried out in excitement. June pushed past them to look over the railing again.

The Slitheen were getting to their feet. They dusted each other down, shaking their heads to clear their senses. Then they looked up at the high rock, looked right up at June, and grinned their wicked grins.

She shuddered with fear, knowing she had nothing left to give, not even able to run away. The Slitheen blinked up at her. And then they threw up their claws.

June followed their gaze, up the slope of the theatre, to where a group of figures stood. Mamps had her claws behind her back, prisoner of the grey blobby aliens who were wielding some kind of ray guns. The Doctor stood with them, looking dishevelled from the fight but otherwise OK. He supervised the blobby aliens as they cuffed Leeb and Cosmo. But as the aliens led their prisoners back up to the cave, the Doctor remained by the TARDIS.

She wanted to call out to him, but couldn't with all

the tourists around her. And he'd said he didn't like goodbyes…

Then a hand clamped down on her shoulder. She turned with a start to see the good-looking guard, some Greek policemen just behind him.

'I'm sorry,' he said. 'But you'll need to answer some questions.'

She denied everything. They sat her under the shade of the Parthenon and brought a cup of tea, but she couldn't explain any of what had happened. Partly, she knew they wouldn't understand. And partly she didn't have the vocabulary. They kept using the word *kostaumi* – they must think the Slitheen had been men in costume.

With a pang of loss, she realised the Doctor must have gone, that she no longer shared his magic ability to understand any language. He had brought her back, just as he'd promised. But she felt awful at not being able to have thanked him for everything she'd seen. Because despite all the horror and exhaustion, she had loved being with him.

The police eventually decided she couldn't help them and agreed to let her go. Knowing it was all over, June walked one last time round the high rock, allowing herself one quick glance down at the ruin of the theatre. The TARDIS still stood there.

June made her way quickly back to the exit, ignoring the good-looking guard as he tried to ask her for a drink. She made her way gingerly along the same path she had now followed so many times before. The last slope took the breath from her, but she would not have dreamt of stopping. She staggered down the uneven steps of the theatre, almost laughing out loud at the site of the blue police box stood there so incongruously. It trembled with strange power as she reached for the door. But it would not open.

June slapped her hands against the wood panels. 'Doctor!' she called. 'Doctor!'

She almost fell in on him when the door creaked open.

'Hello,' he said. 'You took your time.'

'I had to answer some questions.'

He sighed. 'Me too. Had to pop back to the year Arlene-plus-22 and fill in loads of forms. Turns out Cecrops was right. His family has taken the Slitheen business to pieces and got them on all sorts of charges. They couldn't send anyone back to rescue Mamps and the others because the time bus got impounded.'

'So the blobby aliens wanted to arrest Mamps and the others,' she said.

'Yeah,' said the Doctor, awkwardly. 'I sort of got the wrong end of the stick. Nearly ended up with a charge of obstructing justice.'

'But if you hadn't,' said June, 'you wouldn't have met me, we wouldn't have gone back in time, and we wouldn't have stopped the Slitheen in the first place.

'That's what I told them,' said the Doctor. 'Let me off with a warning. I suppose that's OK.'

June grinned at him. 'So it's all worked out,' she said.

But the Doctor looked away into the distance. 'I think so,' he said. 'But at what cost.'

She nodded sadly. 'All those people who died,' she said.

The Doctor looked back at her. 'And you'll have missed your train home.'

She gaped at him for a moment, then quickly checked her watch. Her train would have left more than half an hour before. And the next would miss her connection, so she'd never get back to St Pancras. After everything she'd been through, she wanted to laugh.

'What am I going to do?' she said.

'Well,' said the Doctor. 'I came back because I've still got your rucksack. You'll need your passport to book another train.' His eyes twinkled. 'Or…'

'Or?' she said, already knowing what he was going to ask her.

'Or I could give you a lift.'

She looked him up and down. 'Straight home to Birmingham. No detours.'

'Scout's honour.'

'No answering distress signals? Nothing dangerous or mad?'

'Of course not,' he said. And then he smiled at her. His dark eyes twinkled with mischief.

Laughing, June followed him inside.

Acknowledgements

I've pillaged history and lots of people's hard work to cobble together this story. Cecrops, Aglauros and several other of the characters appear in *The Greek Myths*, as retold by Robert Graves. I used Louise Schofield's *The Mycenaeans* as a guide to 1500 BC, and Mary Beard's *The Parthenon* and Ian Jenkins' *The Parthenon Sculptures* to find my way round the site now and as it was in its heyday.

Ken Dowden's *The Uses of Greek Mythology* explores how the ancient stories have been spun and adapted to suit the needs of each new generation. Three of Dowden's former students – Debbie Challis, Xanna Eve Chown and Scott Handcock – made comments on various bits of this book, catching my more embarrassing errors. Debbie also marched me round the Acropolis telling me clever things and pointed me in the direction of the ancient Greek bits in the British Museum.

Russell T Davies, Rob Francis, Rupert Laight, Gareth Roberts and Gary Russell also spared time to answer questions on the finer points of Slitheen history and culture.

Thanks also to Robert Dick, Amanda Lindsay and Manpreet Sidhu for their assistance. Lastly, thanks to Justin for letting me write the thing, Steve for correcting my spelling, Lee for another amazing cover, and everyone at BBC Books.

DOCTOR · WHO

STING OF THE ZYGONS
by Stephen Cole

THE LAST DODO
by Jacqueline Rayner

WOODEN HEART
by Martin Day

FOREVER AUTUMN
by Mark Morris

SICK BUILDING
by Paul Magrs

WETWORLD
by Mark Michalowski

WISHING WELL
by Mark Morris

THE PIRATE LOOP
by Simon Guerrier

PEACEMAKER
by James Swallow

DOCTOR·WHO

Martha in the Mirror
by Justin Richards
ISBN 978 1 84607 420 2
£6.99

Castle Extremis – whoever holds it can control
the provinces either side that have been at war for
centuries. Now the castle is about to play host to the
signing of a peace treaty. But as the Doctor and Martha
find out, not everyone wants the war to end.

Who is the strange little girl who haunts the castle?
What is the secret of the book the Doctor finds, its
pages made from thin, brittle glass? Who is the hooded
figure that watches from the shadows? And what is the
secret of the legendary Mortal Mirror?

The Doctor and Martha don't have long to find the
answers – an army is on the march, and the castle will
soon be under siege once more…

Also available from BBC Books
featuring the Doctor and Martha
as played by David Tennant and Freema Agyeman:

DOCTOR · WHO

SnowGlobe 7
by Mike Tucker
ISBN 978 1 84607 421 9
£6.99

Earth, 2099. Global warming is devastating the
climate. The polar ice caps are melting.

In a desperate attempt at preservation, the
governments of the world have removed vast sections
of the Arctic and Antarctic and set them inside huge
domes across the world. The Doctor and Martha arrive
in SnowGlobe 7 in the Middle East, hoping for peace
and relaxation. But they soon discover that it's not
only ice and snow that has been preserved beneath the
Dome.

While Martha struggles to help with an infection
sweeping through the Dome, the Doctor discovers an
alien threat that has lain hidden since the last ice age. A
threat that is starting to thaw.

The Nor' Loch is being filled in. If you ask the soldiers
there, they'll tell you it's a stinking cesspool that the
city can do without. But that doesn't explain why the
workers won't go near the place without an armed
guard.

That doesn't explain why they whisper stories about
the loch giving up its dead, about the minister who
walked into his church twelve years after he died…

It doesn't explain why, as they work, they whisper
about a man called the Doctor.

And about the many hands of Alexander Monro.

DOCTOR·WHO

Starships and Spacestations
by Justin Richards
ISBN 978 1 84607 423 3
£7.99

The Doctor has his TARDIS to get him from place to place and time to time, but the rest of the Universe relies on more conventional transport… From the British Space Programme of the late twentieth century to Earth's Empire in the far future, from the terrifying Dalek Fleet to deadly Cyber Ships, this book documents the many starships and spacestations that the Doctor and his companions have encountered on their travels.

He has been held prisoner in space, escaped from the moon, witnessed the arrival of the Sycorax and the crash landing of a space pig… More than anyone else, the Doctor has seen the development of space travel between countless worlds.

This stunningly illustrated book tells the amazing story of Earth's ventures into space, examines the many alien fleets who have paid Earth a visit, and explores the other starships and spacestations that the Doctor has encountered on his many travels…

DOCTOR·WHO

The Doctor Trap

by Simon Messingham

ISBN 978 1 846 07558 0

£6.99

Sebastiene was perhaps once human. He might look like a nineteenth-century nobleman, but in truth he is a ruthless hunter. He likes nothing more than luring difficult opposition to a planet, then hunting them down for sport. And now he's caught them all – from Zargregs to Moogs, and even the odd Eternal…

In fact, Sebastiene is after only one more prize. For this trophy, he knows he is going to need help. He's brought together the finest hunters in the universe to play the most dangerous game for the deadliest quarry of them all.

They are hunting for the last of the Time Lords
– the Doctor.

For Donna Noble, the Andromeda galaxy is a long, long way from home. But even two and a half million light years from Earth, danger lurks around every corner…

A visit to an art gallery turns into a race across space to uncover the secret behind a shadowy organisation.

From the desert world of Karris to the interplanetary scrapyard of Junk, the Doctor and Donna discover that appearances can be deceptive, that enemies are lurking around every corner – and that the centuries-long peace between humans and machines may be about to come to an end.

Because waiting in the wings to bring chaos to the galaxy is the Cult of Shining Darkness.

DOCTOR · WHO

The Time Traveller's Almanac

by Steve Tribe

ISBN 978 1 846 07572 8

£14.99

Who are the eminent artists of the 16th, 19th or 21st centuries? What are the mysteries of Carrionite science? Where do the Daleks come from? Answers to all of these questions and more are found in *The Time Traveller's Almanac*, the ultimate intergalactic fact-finder.

The *Almanac* draws on resources far and wide, from the beginning of time to the end of the universe, to provide information on key historical events and great lives, important issues in science, technology and the arts, and the stories that have defined each era.

Fully illustrated with photos and artwork, *The Time Traveller's Almanac* provides an essential biography of the *Doctor Who* universe.

For a year, while the Master ruled over Earth, Martha
Jones travelled the world telling people stories about
the Doctor. She told people of how the Doctor has
saved them before, and how he will save them again.

This is that story. It tells of Martha's travels from
her arrival on Earth as the Toclafane attacked and
decimated the population through to her return to
Britain to face the Master. It tells how she spread the
word and told people about the Doctor. The story of
how she survived that terrible year.

But it's more than that. This is also a collection of the
stories she tells – the stories of adventures she had with
the Doctor that we haven't heard about before. The
stories that inspired and saved the world…

DOCTOR · WHO

Beautiful Chaos

by Gary Russell

ISBN 978 1 846 07563 6

£6.99

Donna Noble is back home in London, catching
up with her family and generally giving them all
the gossip about her journeys. Her grandfather is
especially overjoyed – he's discovered a new star and
had it named after him. He takes the Doctor, as his
special guest, to the naming ceremony.

But the Doctor is suspicious about some of the other
changes he can see in Earth's heavens. Particularly
that bright star, right there. No, not that one, that one,
there, on the left…

The world's population is slowly being converted to a
new path, a new way of thinking. Something is coming
to Earth, an ancient force from the Dark Times.
Something powerful, angry, and all-consuming…

At the heart of the ruined city of Arcopolis is the Fortress. It's a brutal structure placed here by one of the sides in a devastating intergalactic war that's long ended. Fifteen years ago, the entire population of the planet was killed in an instant by the weapon housed deep in the heart of the Fortress. Now only the ghosts remain.

The Doctor arrives, and determines to fight his way past the Fortress's automatic defences and put the weapon beyond use. But he soon discovers he's not the only person in Arcopolis. What is the true nature of the weapon? Is the planet really haunted? Who are the Eyeless? And what will happen if they get to the weapon before the Doctor?

The Doctor has a fight on his hands. And this time he's all on his own.

Also available from BBC Books
featuring the Doctor
as played by David Tennant:

DOCTOR · WHO

Judgement of the Judoon
by Colin Brake
ISBN 978 1 846 07639 8
£6.99

Elvis the King Spaceport has grown into the sprawling
city-state of New Memphis – an urban jungle, where
organised crime is rife. But the launch of the new
Terminal 13 hasn't been as smooth as expected. And
things are about to get worse...

When the Doctor arrives, he finds the whole terminal
locked down. The notorious Invisible Assassin is at
work again, and the Judoon troopers sent to catch him
will stop at nothing to complete their mission.

With the assassin loose on the mean streets of New
Memphis, the Doctor is forced into a strange alliance.
Together with teenage private eye Nikki and a ruthless
Judoon Commander, the Doctor soon discovers that
things are even more complicated – and dangerous –
than he first thought…